# COWBOY SEEKS A WIFE

EAGLE MOUNTAIN BROTHERS, BOOK 5

MARLEY MICHAELS

# 1

## NORA

Staring out the window of my second-story office, I look out over the green and gold smattered valley of my hometown, Timber Falls. Despite living here for all of my thirty-one years and watching the small mountain town morph from quiet and sleepy to bustling and thriving with development and tourism, I still marvel at how beautiful the scenery is. The snow-capped range that lines one side of the town has a lot to do with it, but the mix of farmland and residential on the other just adds to my love of the place.

And this is where I get to live and work. It may not be everyone's American dream, but it's mine. Living with my mom and my daughter while continuing to build my one-woman accounting business here in town, that's all I need to be happy. There's just one thing missing from my life, but *that's* something I try not to dwell on because I still have so much time ahead of me to make my dreams happen. As my mother always says, the two things you need most in life are patience and time.

A knock on my door grabs my attention, and I turn around just as my assistant pops her head in. "Diana. You finished for the day?" I ask, glancing down at my watch to see it's closing in on four p.m.

"Yeah, is that OK? Everything is all finished up for the week, and the husband is taking me out for dinner and dancing tonight for our anniversary."

I grin at her and nod. "Absolutely. Go. Have a good time and say hi to Paul for me."

"Thanks, Nora. I plan on it," she says with a wink. "And make sure you don't stay too late. I'm sure Leah is waiting at home for you."

Snorting, I shake my head. "I doubt *that*. But let's check, shall we?" The very *last* thing my darling sixteen-year-old daughter will do right now is wait at home where she's supposed to be. Whoever said that kids will be the light of your life also forgot to mention all the premature gray hairs they cause when they're teenagers and think they know everything. I pull my cell phone out of my pocket and swipe the screen open, bringing up my Life 360 app that Leah and I both have to track each other.

"Aha! See!" I cross the room and show the phone to my amused assistant. "She's currently at the playground in the town square, no doubt hanging out with her new boyfriend, Heath... or is it Dale... or Cash..." I can't keep up with the ever-changing relationship status of my teenager these days.

Diana's eyes are dancing with mirth now. "I'd say like mother like daughter, but I *do* want to get out of here," she teases, earning my poked-out tongue.

"Off with you. And I promise I'll leave as soon as I've finished the monthly accounts for Eagle Mountain ranch."

"*Actually*... that's quite timely..." she says suspiciously. "Because Randy Barnes called and said he needed an urgent appointment. He insisted it *had* to be before the weekend."

My heart jumps at the sound of his name. Randy has not only been my client for a few years now, but he's also the only man who has caught my eye and had me thinking of things that could never be—not with *him*. Not with a woman like me, anyway.

"OK..." I say slowly, knowing he lives an hour away. "Can you ask him to maybe email his request through to me? By the time he gets here from the ranch, it'll be after five."

Diana shakes her head. "He's in town and said he can be here in ten minutes." She looks down at her watch. "Which is right about—" That's when the elevator dings and the sound of the old squeaking doors opening reach my ears. Her gaze is apologetic. "About *now*, actually."

I huff out a sigh but shoot her a smile. "Thanks, Diana. If you could just send him through and then go home and get yourself ready for your night out. That's an order."

"You're the best, Nora. Don't stay too late, you hear?"

"Yes, M*om*," I say with a laugh, waving her goodbye as she steps out of view.

I quickly look myself up and down, smoothing my clammy hands down my gray pencil skirt and checking my white blouse in the window reflection. It's been a long day—a long *week*—but I still find myself wanting to look my best for Mr. Barnes.

Then I quickly move behind my desk, wondering if I should sit down in my chair or grab the Eagle Mountain Ranch file from the cabinet.

Just as I decide to grab the file and bend over with my butt facing the door to pull it out of the drawer, a low grunt sounds from behind me, my back going ramrod straight, my head going smack against the edge of the cabinet on the way up.

"*Fuck*," I curse, dropping the file as my hand jerks to rub my hair, all while turning around in my black kitten heels and meeting the wide eyes of Randy Barnes, my biggest client and the most handsome man I've ever met. With a big, brawny body, dark hair, and a thick trimmed beard, he's the very definition of a handsome, manly *man. At least to me, anyway.* I like to imagine him picking me up and slinging me over his shoulder caveman style, but that's not exactly appropriate accountant/client behavior.

Randy removes his Stenson as he steps forward like he's about to reach for me, but stops himself, his hands dropping back to his side. "Sorry, Nora. Your assistant told me to come straight through." He frowns. "You OK?"

*I'm dying of embarrassment, but fake it till you make it, right?*

"Yep. Fine. I mean..." I take a breath. "Sorry. Yes, I'm good. Great, even. Would you like to sit down?" I ramble, bending down to grab the dropped file before standing and moving back behind my desk.

His gaze studies me for a beat before he shakes his head and moves to the seat opposite me, not once taking his eyes off me. "I apologize for the late notice, but something has come up that needs my urgent attention." Now that gets *my* attention.

I slide my chair in closer and open the folder. "OK, Randy. What's the problem?"

"Earlier this year, the ranch was gifted a rodeo bull by my soon-to-be sister-in-law's parents. And believin' that he came to us free and clear—"

"As a gift usually is…"

He nods. "Exactly. Thinkin' he was now owned by us and the ranch, we had him checked and when we got the all-clear, we put him out to stud with our best cows to sire calves."

"As you would. It's how you make a buck."

"Yeah. But now one of the rodeo owners has come to us intimating that the bull is, in fact, part of a business arrangement—a partnership —between us and the rodeo."

My head jerks back, and I flip through the documents in the folder in front of me. "I don't have any paperwork about any ownership agreements for bulls. You haven't used other bulls to sire calves in many years, from what I remember."

"That's right, we haven't. And we would never have bred with him had we known that this was the expectation. Now, Ron Moore, one of the rodeo owners, is demanding we provide fully grown bulls to the rodeo free of charge whenever they need them. I explained that's not gonna happen because raisin' a bull calf ain't free, and the gift of the bull was more of a cost to us in upkeep and care than it was a gain. But he ain't hearin' it. He's got it in his head that since the bull was the best they had, then he should somehow make our calves more valuable. The man has zero understandin' of how cattle ranchin' works and is being as bull-headed as the bull he gave us."

"And just to confirm, you never signed anything resembling an agreement or contract outlining the ownership transfer of the bull? Or any financial details as to what would happen with the sired calves when they were born?"

"Nope. Not at all."

I lean back in my chair, clasping my hands on the desk in front of me, and looking over at the ruggedly handsome rancher. "What about any kind of gentleman's agreement? Verbal promises, shaken hands, or the like?"

"Nora, you know that's not how I run my business. If there's any money or costs involved when it comes to the ranch, it's signed, sealed, and delivered, or no dice. I don't budge on that, not since we've been workin' so hard on gettin' the ranch to where we want it to be—where it *is* now."

"Yes, I know. But it would be remiss of me not to ask. I hope you understand."

He nods, his gaze growing intense as he stares back at me. "I do, and that's why I wanted to get started on gatherin' as much information about this as possible. Which is where you come in."

I shoot him a smile—a professional one, of course. "What do you want me to do?"

His eyes darken for just a second, but he quickly schools his expression. It's almost as if I was imagining a look of... *something*... crossing his features. "I think we should start with a costing schedule that outlines the cost of keepin' and raisin' bull calves, as well as the ongoin' expenses involved with keeping the sire—Big Bruiser—on the ranch. We need to show that the gift is actually a liability more than anything else."

Grabbing a pen, I quickly jot down some notes on the lined pad next to me.

"OK. I'm gathering by your last-minute appointment that these are pressing matters?"

"You know me, Nora. I always want to be prepared."

"Information gathering in anticipation of a fight?" I reply, a little—OK, maybe a lot—too flirty for a professional conversation.

That's when Randy's lips quirk up on one side, stealing all the breath I have in my chest. "Somethin' like that," he muses, his gaze dropping to my mouth before his body tenses and his eyes jerk back up to mine.

*Wait... did he just... no. Surely not...*

Time to end this before I do something like *flirt* with him again. I push my chair back and near on jump to my feet, wobbling a bit as my equilibrium struggles to catch up with my change of position. "OK, Randy. That's something I can do for you. When would you need this report by?"

Ever the gentleman he's always shown himself to be, he stands to his full height, looking down at me, his hat cradled in his hand. "I have a phone call with Ron and Phil Moore in the middle of next week. Is that too soon? I don't wanna intrude on your weekend, of course."

I snort, earning furrowed brows from the man. *Push past it. The man doesn't need to know that I have no social life and a teenager who would rather socialize with friends than hang out with her mother.* "I can make a start on it over the weekend, and if you can come back on Tuesday, I can go over the report with you so that you've got all the information you need for your call."

"Tuesday. Sounds good, Nora." He moves to leave and for the first time, I'm disappointed he's going so soon. *Maybe I'm just feeling a little lonely today, that must be it.*

Before I can respond, he stops in the doorway, lifting one of his strong bulging arms to place his black suede Stetson on top of his head before glancing my way.

"Could you make it the last appointment of the day? We are knee-deep in ranch work at the moment, so if I'm traveling all this way, I wouldn't mind taking you out for a meal to say thank you for giving up some of your weekend to help."

My whole body stills as my brain struggles to process his words, but my pulse spikes and I swear for a moment that I can *feel* my blood coursing through my veins... *everywhere. Did Randy Barnes just ask me on a date? Surely I misheard him...* Before I find the ability to conjugate, he continues. "I mean, a business dinner. But I understand if you have other commitments." If anything, Randy looks just as tightly wound as I'm feeling, which is kind of endearing and sweet but also confusing as all get out. Randy Barnes is *not* indecisive. He's determined and strong-willed and never in all the years I've worked for him has he ever seemed... unsure.

"Yes," I blurt out, wanting to put the both of us out of our misery. "Yes. I can do that—a business dinner, that is."

The slow-growing smile curves his lips and is breathtaking in its beauty. Which is saying something when the man doing it is every inch the rugged, burly, bearded mountain man I read about in all of my romance novels. If ever there was a man who epitomizes every fictional hero I've ever imagined, it would be him.

"Good. I won't keep you any longer, Nora. Have a good weekend. See you next week." He tips his hat my way before disappearing, leaving me to do a little happy dance over our 'business dinner', because no matter what name you call it, I'm going to shower and shave as if this is a date. I'd thought there was no chance for a single mother with a past like mine to even get a look in with a man like Randy Barnes. So if this is my one chance to wow him, I'm going all out. I'm going to make him wonder how he ever lived a day without me.

## 2

## RANDY

"What's that nice smell?" my sister, Ellie-Mae, asks as I step out of my room, freshly showered and ready to hit the road.

"I showered and put on a little cologne. It ain't no sin," I grunt, as I make it down the end of the hall and enter the kitchen, stopping in the entryway to adjust the tie around my neck. *Why are these things so damn uncomfortable?*

Ellie's eyes move from my face down to my clothing, clocking the button-up shirt, slacks, and freshly shined dress shoes. "And what on earth are you wearin'? Did someone die that I don't know about?"

Scowling, I tug the tie loose and pull it free from around my neck. "I have a business meetin', that's all," I grumble, shoving the tie into my pocket as I try to move past her to get my coat.

"Fancy business meetin'," she says, stepping closer to me and holding her hand out. "Want me to sort that tie out for you?"

I shake my head. "I think I'll just skip it."

"You sure? Don't want you to be the only guy there without a tie on. They'll think us ranchers don't know how to operate in polite society."

"There won't be other men," I say, pulling my jacket out of the hall cupboard and shrugging into it. It's a little tight across the back. I'm obviously a little broader than I was the last time I wore it.

"Oh. So...only women, then? Or...maybe just *one* woman?" Ellie's interested eyes study me carefully, doing her usual in trying to glean information from the things I *don't* say.

In all the years she's been with us—Ellie-Mae is more of an adopted sister than a blood relative who stayed with our family after her daddy passed away unexpectedly—I don't think I've ever wished for her to be anywhere but in the ranch house. Normally, she's a happy face, ready with a cup of cowboy coffee, a slice of pie and some good conversation. But today, I'd rather keep to myself.

I level her with a cool stare, warning her off-topic before I speak. "It's business, Ellie-Mae. Just business."

"OK. You enjoy your *business* meetin' then," she says, lifting both hands in the air like she's surrendering. Problem is, the tiny smile at the corner of her mouth is telling me she's unlikely to let this drop. She's sniffed out a bone, and she'll keep digging until she finds it. I don't want her to find this. The meeting—the *dinner*—I'm having with Nora under the *guise* of business isn't something I'm ready to share with the family yet. I need to keep it to myself. At least until I understand exactly what *it* is.

"Don't wait up," I say, softening my voice as I grab my keys and head for the door.

"Be sure to compliment her hairstyle or somethin'," Ellie-Mae calls after me, causing me to chuckle as I let out a sigh and close the door behind me. There's no hiding *anything* from that woman.

"Where are you off to?" my brother, Beau, asks as he emerges from the barn and finds me walking toward my truck looking more banker than rancher.

"Business meetin'," I grunt in his direction.

"Better you than me."

"See you when I'm through," I say, getting into my truck and smiling to myself over the difference between my brother's line of questioning and my sister's. I guess men really are simple creatures.

Starting my engine, I make my way down the long drive that connects the ranch with the road and try to ignore the nerves swirling about in my gut. As far as Nora is concerned, this date isn't a date at all. I asked her out to talk *business,* but even then, I knew I wanted this night to mean more.

Ever since our old accountant retired, and Nora took over his business, I've felt a...spark between us. She's the kind of woman who not only looks good but has the intellect, sense of humor and get up and go that most people can only dream about having. What she's doing working in a tiny backwater accounting firm when she could be making it big in a city like Anchorage is beyond me, but I sure am grateful that she's here. Her expertise has been one of the main factors in pulling the ranch out of financial ruin and into profit in just a few short years. I owe her a debt of gratitude, and if she's willing, I'd like to be a lot more than just grateful to her. I'd like to date her too.

But would a woman as intelligent and cultured as her even look twice at a rancher like me?

It's something I aim to find out at our meeting, and while I'm kicking myself for being too chicken shit to ask her out directly, I do plan on being a little more direct with the beautiful Nora tonight. Over the years, I've gotten a sense that she's just as interested in me as I am in her, but there's always something holding us back. For her, it might just be the fact that I'm her client and it would be unprofessional. And for me, it's been a little—well, *big*—thing called the 'Mountain's Call'.

You see, the Call, simply put, is a reward. It's born from the spiritual connection that my family and our ancestors have with the land we raise our cattle on, and for those of us who live and work on the land, the spirit inside the Mountain *calls* the woman to our side who will make us whole—our soulmate.

And I know it sounds like a bunch of hocus pocus, but I've watched all of my siblings and one of my cousins receive the Mountain's Call so far. They're all as happy as pigs in shit, and I'm happy for them in return. But...I'm also lonely as fuck.

Being the oldest of all of us, it's been a hard thing to witness my brothers and now my cousins receive the Call before me. When we learned what it was from Ellie-Mae's husband, Miller, we felt certain I'd be the first. But four Barnes men in and I'm still waiting. I'm not jealous. I know my time will come when my soulmate is ready, but I am impatient. Hell, I'm a forty-eight-year-old man who's gonna run out of time to have a family if it takes much longer than it already has, so as a man of action, I've decided to take matters into my own hands. It's time I make the Call come to me.

It's not like the Call hasn't worked that way in the past. My cousin, Jasper, didn't even know if he was going to hear the Call from the Mountain Spirit. So he tested it out and threw everything he had at a burgeoning relationship with his now-fiancée, Sarah. And that paid off just fine since they're head over heels and planning a wedding a month from now. So, after watching him negotiate *his* Call in a less than traditional way, I've decided it's time to give *my* Call a helping hand too. And tonight, that starts with a dinner...

# 3

## NORA

Standing in my bathroom I'm wearing a fluffy white robe and just my bra and underwear beneath—matching of course, and this may be a business date, but I've always had a thing for feeling good when I'm looking good—I can't ignore the butterflies in my tummy.

Don't get me wrong, I'm not delusional and I know this couldn't possibly be a *date* date to Randy Barnes, but to me, it's an opportunity to go out and enjoy adult conversation with someone who isn't a family member. And it's Randy... There's no way I would ever *not* go out of my way and put in a bit of extra effort when I *know* I'm going to be sharing a meal with the man.

Because... it's *him*. A woman's allowed to imagine and fantasize a little, right?

"Now *that's* a rather *risqué* outfit for a *business* dinner, Eleanor," Mom announces from the doorway behind me. "Although I must say, for a thirty-one-year-old working mother, you definitely can pull that off, lovely."

I meet her eyes in the mirror and shimmy my butt her way. "Nice to know you think your daughter still has it."

Mom narrows her gaze. "You're gorgeous and a total catch for any man."

"Not too sure about *that*, Ma."

"Well, I am," she says, her tone leaving no room for doubt. She steps back and turns to look over at the array of clothes laid out all over my bed. "But really, what *are* you wearing? Because there are enough clothes here to fit out the Timber Threads clothing store *and* the town's female population."

Rolling my eyes, I give my lashes one last coat of mascara before standing up straight and giving my makeup a final look over, happy with the smokey-sultry eyes and crimson lip look I decided to go with. Especially since the darker eyes make my green eyes and brunette hair pop even more in the light. With a spritz of my favorite perfume, the subtle scent of jasmine and gardenias filling my senses, I spin on the ball of my foot and follow Mom into my bedroom.

I stand next to her, both of us looking down at the array of outfits covering my comforter. "I was thinking the—"

"Black pencil skirt, blue blouse, that silver necklace Leah and I gave you for Christmas last year—the one that hangs low, and..." She taps her chin, thinking hard before moving to my closet, bending over and coming back to me with my pair of black slingbacks hanging from her fingers. "These. *Definitely* these. They'll make any man—I mean *business* client—take notice."

"*Mom...*" I warn, my light tone giving away my amusement.

She shakes her head. "Don't you *Mom* me. You don't think I completely see through you, daughter dearest?"

"It *is* a business dinner," I implore.

"Mmm hmm..."

"No really, Mom. I'm meeting him there. That's all the proof you need. It's business, not pleasure. I guess I'm just excited about doing something grown-up and *normal* for a change."

She meets my eyes, her gaze narrowing before huffing out a resigned sigh. "*Fine*. But I do think that whoever this *meeting* is with will have his boots knocked off with how pretty you're looking."

I shoot her a gentle smile. "You have to say that. You're my mom."

"I do*n't* have to say anything of the sort. Mom's tell you if you look ridiculous. They tell you if you're heading for disaster. They do *not* tell you you're going to impress any damn one you see out of some maternal obligation." She steps forward and cups my shoulder. "You're gorgeous, successful, and so damn driven. Any available man with a pulse and common sense will take one look at you and know you're a diamond to be treasured and adored. The only one who needs to believe that, my sweet, is *you*."

My throat tightens, my chest heavy with emotion. "Stop. You'll make me ruin my makeup."

Mom's lips tip up, her eyes sparkling. "Well, now, we can't have *that*."

"Thanks, you know. You're the best goddamn cheerleader a girl can have."

"That's all part of the job description. Now, you finished getting dressed, and then come out and give me a look at the whole package before you leave. You never know, Leah might even get home in time to see you off."

I snort and shake my head. "And pigs might fly over the damn mountain top."

"*That* is something I'd love to see," she says with a grin before placing the heels on the bed and walking out of my room.

Turning my attention back to the bed, I decide to go with Mom's suggestion and start getting dressed in the skirt, blouse, and slingbacks. When I'm done, I stand in front of my full-length mirror and take in the whole look.

I may only be thirty-one, but sleepless nights, a teenager hell-bent on making me turn gray prematurely, and everyday life stress have definitely taken their toll, but rather than lament the changes in my looks as I slowly but surely get older, I wear them with pride. Yeah, life hasn't been easy at times, but it's been *real*, and I'm proud of every single thing I've done and achieved—the home Mom and I have, my daughter, my career, all of it. But I miss adult companionship.

Since Friday, in between working on the costings report for Randy, stealing time with Leah —when she's home, that is—and doing all the normal boring errands adults have to do, I've found myself imagining what would happen if this dinner with Randy *wasn't* just for business.

Would he have picked me up, coming to my door with a bunch of flowers, opening the car door for me, resting his hand on the small of my back as he led me into the restaurant?

Would he choose a back corner table, giving us some privacy so that we could flirt and laugh as we shared our life stories and funny anecdotes, all with an undertone of wanting more, that whole undercurrent of nervousness and anticipation lacing our every word?

*God, if only!*

"Get yourself together, Nora. It's a *business* dinner. All business. Nothing else," I tell myself as I grab my purse from the top of my dresser and sling it over my shoulder, checking the time and realizing that I really need to hit the road if I want to get to the restaurant on time. It would definitely be unprofessional to be late.

I walk out into the kitchen to find Mom standing at the stove, finishing up what smells like Beef Goulash, my favorite childhood meal —and now Leah's. "Now that's just cruel."

She looks over her shoulder and grins at me. "I don't know what you're talking about. You're getting to go out and eat gourmet 'business dinner' food. I figured the *least* I could do was make my darling granddaughter a good stomach-sticking dinner."

"You're just trying to sweeten her up," I say with a laugh, just as the sound of the front door opening and closing reaches my ears. "Speak of the devil."

"I heard that!" Leah announces as she walks into the room, looking me over with a curious yet cursory glance before moving to her grandmother and kissing her cheek, glancing down at the saucepan with a grin. "Knew I came home for a good reason."

"You mean *not* because that's where teenagers with homework to do and chores to finish *should* be?" I tease.

Leah rolls her eyes, shooting me a smirk. "Well, it looks like *you* won't even be here tonight, so what does it matter *where* I am, Nora?" I grit my teeth, fighting against every urge to take the bait that my increasingly antagonistic daughter tries to lay out for me.

I shake my head. "Totally not going there, sweetheart. But it's lovely to see you home. How was school?"

Leah grunts and shrugs, before moving to the kitchen counter and hefting herself up to sit on top of it. Mom's eyes dart to mine, her look telling me *not* to react. *Easier said than done, Mom.*

"It was school. Where *are* you going, anyway? You look like you're on your way out to hook yourself a sugar daddy." My mouth drops open, but she keeps going. "Although, that's cool. At least then you could stop working and we could all live a life of luxury." She scrunches her nose up. "Unless he's old and wrinkly. Then maybe Nanny could be a better option for him."

"Leah!" I say, my mind blown. Is it true that teenagers can turn from sweet little girls into rampaging monsters overnight? Because I tell you, hormones and surly belligerence have nothing on my daughter.

"What?" She feigns innocence, but my devilish daughter knows what she's doing. "I'm just saying."

"For your information, I have a *business* dinner. I told you about it last night, remember?"

"While we were watching that boring cooking show?" I nod. "Yeah, I had my headphones in. I kind of didn't hear a word of what y'all were saying."

My eyes bug out, and I have to bite my cheek not to reply. *Moving forward...*

"*Anyway*, I'm gonna go have a shower and ring Jacob before dinner. Have fun with the sugar daddy, Mother dearest." Then, just like that, she's strutting down the hall and out of sight.

I watch her go before turning back to Mom. "*Please* tell me I was nothing like that."

Mom smirks and arches a brow. "Do you forget that there are sixteen years between you and your daughter, my sweet?"

I sigh, because yes, that really does say it all.

"But don't you worry about her. You best be going." I nod, my nerves returning full force now. "And have *fun*. Maybe suggest a nightcap afterward," she says with a wink.

"Mom!"

"What? You're thirty-one, not *dead*. You haven't been out on a date in years. Live it up. You'll never know unless you try. Remember that."

And those are the words running through my head as I say goodbye and make my way out of the house to my car.

*You'll never know unless you try.*

Well, Randy Barnes. Let's see what the night brings, shall we?

# 4

# RANDY

I arrive too early, and when the hostess takes me to a private table in the back corner I start to panic that Nora is going to come in here and feel like I tricked her into a date under the guise of a business meeting. Which really, is exactly what I did. But I don't need to be so damn obvious *about it.*

"Ah, can we get a table that's a bit more in the middle of things?" I ask, taking in the ambient lighting and the single rose decorating the table.

"You requested a quiet spot in the restaurant, sir. This is the best we have. If we put you in the thick of things it won't be so quiet anymore." She looks at me with big, confused eyes and just blinks.

"I'm aware of what I requested. I just..." Releasing a sigh, I lift my hand and pinch the bridge of my nose between my thumb and forefinger. "It doesn't need to be *this* quiet and secluded. I don't want my companion to get the wrong idea.."

The young girl looks at me and blinks a little more. "Um.. what's the message you're trying to send here? Because all of this"—she waves her arm over the center of the table—"says to me that you're trying to impress her. "

"I... I, um..." Crap. I have no idea what I'm doing here. I haven't been on a dinner date with a woman for so long that I think I've forgotten how to do this. Now I've gone and chosen the fanciest restaurant in Timber Falls and the most romantic table they have, proving I should've just manned up and asked Nora out directly. My biggest fear is that I've misread all the signs and Nora is going to come here expecting a business meeting and nothing but a business meeting which is going to make me look mighty foolish and possibly end with me needing to find another accountant. Something I don't want to do. Suddenly my usually unflappable self is feeling more than a little flapped. *Fuck. I might have made a terrible error here.*

"Randy?"

The scent of jasmine and gardenias touches my nose before I spin around and find Nora standing behind me, looking like an absolute knockout in a black pencil skirt and pale blue blouse. My eyes travel down to her feet, the low strappy heels giving me ideas I have no right to. In particular, those shoes on her naked legs slung over my shoulders are *absolutely* the kind of thoughts a man should keep to himself unless until at least the third date. In the case of business meetings—pretend or otherwise—those thoughts should never see the light of day.

My gaze flies right back up to hers before my dick grabs hold of that idea and responds accordingly. "Nora. Hey." I don't know if I should hug her, kiss her cheek, or shake her hand. So I do this weird kind of elbow grab before almost head-butting her. I pull back sharply. "Sorry...Can I get you something to drink?"

"That'd be great. White wine, please?" she says to the hostess who is standing by, obviously unsure of the table situation still.

"Did you still want to change the table, sir?" she asks as Nora moves toward her seat.

*Shit, the table.* "Ah, no. Thank you. It's fine," I say, pulling Nora's chair out for her like the gentleman I was raised to be. "Thank you."

"Of course. Can I get a drink for you as well?"

"Wine is fine for me too," I reply, moving to the other side of the table and sitting across from

Nora. The Hostess moves away, leaving us on our own and Nora turns her pretty face to me, her cheeks flushed as she smiles broadly.

"This is lovely." Her gaze roams over the table before lifting to mine. "And you scrub up well, Randy." Do I tell her I think she's beautiful? Is that a business kind of thing to do? Before I can decide, she continues, and for the first time, it hits me that Nora might be nervous, too. "I don't think I've ever eaten here before."

"Me either. So if the food is awful, I apologize in advance."

Nora giggles as she takes her napkin and lies it across her lap. I copy the movement. "I'm sure it will be fine. My receptionist, Diana, comes here with her husband on special occasions. She says that their gnocchi is to die for."

"Well, then. I'll take Diana's advice under advisement. A good gnocchi is hard to find."

"My mother makes a really good one. And an amazing goulash. She was tempting me with it when I left tonight."

"You live with your mother?" I ask, grabbing onto any bit of personal information she offers. When her cheeks flush, those damn nerves twist up my guts again. *Am I fucking this up?* I'm a man who likes things to be direct and concise. I like people to know exactly where they stand with me, which is why I'm starting to regret trying to blur the lines here. I wanted this to be a date, and I should've just manned up and come right out and said what it was—what I *wanted* it to be—from the start. This middle-of-the-road business is making me an overthinking, bumbling mess. *Real impressive Randy.*

"Ah, yeah. Lame, right? I'm in my 30s and my mom is still making me dinner and helping run my life. I'd probably be considered as one of those people who failed to launch in a lot of circles."

"Failed to launch? I don't even know what that means."

"It just means that you didn't grow up, move out of home and separate yourself from your family the way most other people would. You know, cut the apron strings."

"Jesus. If that's what constitutes a failure to launch, then I guess you can consider me one too. I still live in the house I was born in, my entire family helps to run every aspect of my life, and my little sister makes most of my meals."

"I think it's a bit different when your family owns and runs a ranch, Randy."

"No," I say with a shake of my head. "I don't think it is. From where I'm sittin', you're a successful woman who's choosin' to stay close to family. There's no shame in that. More people should."

Nora tilts her head as she looks over at me. "I suppose you're right. Maybe calling it a failure to launch is a little harsh."

"Definitely. I reckon that term is probably reserved for high school dropouts livin' in their parents' basements and contributin' nothin', right?"

Her answering smile dazzles me. "I'm definitely not in the basement. Mom and I, we actually bought the house together."

"Well, that's what I call keepin' it in the family. But then, I've been told many times that ranchers and regular folk tend to do things a little different."

"I happen to like the way you do things, Randy. You have a lot of people to look out for, and you've worked really hard to make it so you can."

"I didn't do it on my own, Nora. Your work helped enormously. I honestly wouldn't be where I am if it wasn't for your guidance."

A small smile plays on the edge of her lips. "Which is what this dinner is about, right? A thank you for the work?"

"Yeah. Of course." Her eyes drop a little and I feel like maybe I just said the wrong thing. But I don't get the chance to correct it before the waiter arrives at our table with a bottle of chilled wine. He makes a big show of opening it and getting me to taste it and approve it. I have no fucking clue what I'm doing here, so I just nod and wait for him to fill our glasses. And by the time he's finally done, the moment seems to have evaporated with Nora reaching into her bag and pulling out a cream-colored folder.

"We should probably get this part out of the way before it's time to order," she says, giving me a small smile before launching into explaining the cost analysis she's put together. And as the numbers and explanations leave her pretty pink lips, that line I blurred becomes a little clearer. This *is* a business dinner, and it seems like I've already lost any chance I had of changing that. Damn it.

## 5

## NORA

There was a moment before our food arrived where I could've sworn Randy and I were having a non-business dinner type of conversation. But then I had to open my big mouth and ruin whatever mood was building by hauling out the damn costing analysis I'd done.

After that, through appetizers then the mains—an Alaskan crab bisque with a side of toasted garlic sourdough for me, wagyu tomahawk steak with potato mash and steamed greens for Randy—the conversation stayed very much on the business side. It was all about animals, feed schedules, land regeneration, and plans to expand the horse rescue center they'd created with his sister-in-law, Kendra, who's married to his brother, Jesse.

And it was all very friendly and nice, not at all awkward or stilted. *That* kind of conversation I can do with my eyes closed and my hands tied behind my back. Business, accounting, cost-projections,\ and future financial planning are all bread and butter, my stable, go-to topics that I probably defer to a *bit* too much when in the company of other adults. But that's just me, I guess. I'm all work, all mom and daughter. I promised myself when Leah was born that I'd give her the best life possible—and I'd like to think I've achieved that. But obviously, that meant not giving myself any time to be a woman who could date and put herself out there while holding a *normal* or even flirtatious conversation. It's possible I lost that skill long broken, or perhaps it never really had a chance to develop since I had my daughter when I was only sixteen.

When the waiter comes to clear our empty plates away and asks if we want to see the dessert menu, I'm a little *too* eager when I tell him I do, earning an arched brow and twitching grin from my dinner companion.

"Got a bit of a sweet tooth, Nora?" he asks, leaning into his arms resting on the table.

I smirk. "Maybe. How about you?"

Randy's eyes flash wide before growing hooded, and damn if that flash of heat I catch in his gaze doesn't do delightful things to my insides. "I never say no to somethin' sweet when it's on offer."

*Holy god. I think I'm dead... or dreaming... maybe I'm dreaming* and *I'm dead*. Randy Barnes just *totally* flirted with me... right? *Right???*

Before I can even stop myself, I mimic his stance and lean into the table. "The sweeter, the better."

The smile Randy gives me is so disarmingly sexy, I feel a little lightheaded. "We've discussed the ranch backward and forward throughout dinner. So, how about we use dessert to learn a little more about each other as people?"

I have to bite the inside of my cheek to stop myself from smiling too wide. "I'd like that very much."

"Me too." His eyes shine brightly as he lifts his wine glass and drains the final sip. "I'll start with something easy. Besides dessert, what else do you like?" he asks.

"Hmm. I'm a sucker for a good coffee. Two sugars, of course."

He sits back and nods. "My sister makes the best damn coffee in all the district. It's so strong she swears it puts hairs on *her* chest."

A startled laugh bubbles out of me. "No wonder you work so hard over there at the ranch. You've got straight caffeine running through your veins. Maybe she should bottle the stuff and sell it? That would be the diversification you've been looking for." I winch a little since I just went immediately to business talk, but Randy doesn't seem to mind. He chuckles and the sound of it is like a warm fluffy blanket I just wanna roll myself up in.... preferably naked. *No, don't go there, Nora.*

"I'll have to pitch the idea to her. She's pretty busy with a toddler and a baby on the way."

"Oh wow. So she's married too?"

"Yes, ma'am. Miller came to stay with us a few years back, and those two hit it off right away. They live in a rebuilt cottage on the ranch, but Ellie's the mother hen of the family, so she looks after all of us brothers and cousins too."

"That's amazing."

"She's one of a kind, that's for sure," he says affectionately. God, does this man have *any* faults? He's hard-working, driven, and a loyal family man who rocks the hell out of a pair of wrangler jeans just as much as the dress pants he's wearing now. The way he talks about his family is something I've always found admirable. They're not a burden to him. He genuinely loves living and working with his kin.

The waiter returns with the dessert menus, and straight away, I know I'm ordering the chocolate brownie with vanilla bean ice cream. Randy orders the same and then we're alone again.

"So Nora, I know you're a financial guru, but what do you like to do when you're not working?" he asks, giving me his full attention.

"I'm pretty much a homebody."

"There sure ain't nothing wrong with that."

"Sometimes it just seems like I work all day, then go home and just muck around the house. I do like my gardens, though. Mom and I have a mini-orchard growing in the backyard that's taken a lot of years and hard work to get growing. Nothing as exciting as living on a ranch, though. What's a few fruit trees when you've got thousands of hectares of pasture and far-too-many-to count head of cattle?"

He chuckles and runs a hand through his hair. "I dunno about that. A lot of people think it's a pretty mundane, boring life."

"Does that matter, though?"

Randy's head jerks, his eyes flashing wide. "What do you mean?"

"Does it matter what other people think? It's your life. Some might say that working at Eagle Mountain on your family land is your destiny.

So why care about anyone else's opinion about something that makes you happy and fulfilled? Which I know it does because there's never been a question over your passion for what you do."

His dark molasses eyes melt right in front of me, and believe me, that is a sight to behold. It gives me images of him staring down at me in bed with a look so hot, so gone with lust that I'd —*Shit, don't go there. At least not until you're alone in bed later...*

But the look in his eyes makes me think I've said something meaningful that he didn't expect, and I like that I've surprised him.

"That's pretty insightful of you, Nora. And you're right. I guess there just comes a time in a man's life—probably a woman's as well—when you start to realize what's missin'."

He's *so* not wrong about that. What I wouldn't give to be the missing piece of the Randy Barnes's puzzle.

His dry laugh fills the air. "Listen to me, an old man moanin' about life when he's got nothin' to complain about. Isn't that great date conversation?"

"Is that what this is?" I blurt out before I can stop myself.

Randy frowns at me. "Is this what?"

"A date." He goes completely still, his expression almost comical. It's like I've just caught him with his hand in the cookie jar or something. "Sorry, I shouldn't have said anything," I mutter, suddenly feeling self-conscious.

"Don't apologize. To be honest, that's been like a monkey on my back ever since I asked you. Is this a date? Does she think it's all business? Should I have just flat out asked her out for a dinner date so that we can get to know each other a little better outside of being client and accountant..."

My mouth drops open until he clenches his jaw shut, and I'm left staring at him stunned silent, something he mistakes badly.

"Shit. I'm sorry, Nora," he says, his hand shooting out to cover mine on the table, a buzz of energy jolting between us the moment his skin touches mine. "I shouldn't have said any of that. I'm sorry. Now you probably think I've brought you here under false pretenses. I apologize."

I stare down at my hand, a slow-burning heat warming my skin where his palm still touches my fingers, my blood pumping so loud that it's ringing in my ears, and my heart is throwing itself against the wall of my chest with reckless abandon. *What in the world is happening to me?* Maybe I'm having some sort of allergic reaction to the crab or something, and it's made me hallucinate? Because I could've sworn Randy Barnes... the man who I've been lusting over for years, just told me he misled me into thinking this was a business date...

"Nora?" He says my name again, and this time when I pin my gaze to his, I see a little sliver of vulnerability I've never once seen in Randy before, and damn if it doesn't touch me deep inside.

"So, this wasn't a business dinner?"

"It was... but it also wasn't." My frown deepens. "Dammit." He pulls his hand from mine and runs it across his bearded face. "What I *mean* is, I did need to get that costing analysis report from you and we obviously needed to discuss that at length—"

"Which we did..."

"Yes. Which we did. But I also wanted it to be a date... "

My eyes roam over his face. He genuinely looks a little guilty and worried over this. "And you didn't think that's something you should've told me?"

"I see now I should've done that, yes. "

If this was any other man, I'd probably make them squirm a little before putting them at ease. But the sincerity in Randy's expression has me wanting to reassure him. "OK."

Randy tilts his head, his brows knitted so tight I'm surprised he can still see straight. "OK?"

I shrug. "Yeah. OK. It probably would've saved me a hell of a lot of time agonizing over what to wear, what message it was sending, and whether this *was* a 'date' date or just a business meeting with food. But it sounds to me like you've been doing a fair amount of your own agonizing and overthinking about this dinner, too. So I'd say we're pretty even, don't you?"

He nods, his smile still wary, but a lot more relaxed than I've seen him all night. It warms my heart to know that this big, burly, rough, and tough rancher was nervous about our date that neither one of us knew was a date. It kind of makes us more alike than I realized.

"How about this, Randy Barnes? We can call this a business dinner"—he opens his mouth as if to argue but I press on–"so you can write it off as a business expense." I shoot him a wink and earn a surprised chuckle from him. "But we'll call this next part a dessert date."

"I like the way you're thinkin'," he says, lifting his wineglass again but realizing it's empty. "Although I have one more question."

"What's that?"

"If I *were* to ask you out again, should I do it as a —" He doesn't get to finish his question because that's the exact moment the waiter returns with our check. And going by the conflicted look on Randy's face, I can't work out if he welcomes the distraction or not because he falls quiet for a moment.

And that just leaves me almost choking on the what if... because where do we go from here? Was he just testing the waters, or does he genuinely want a real date together? Should I bring it up myself or just wait it out and see what he does? Or do I just bite the bullet and ask him right now, putting myself out there and ignoring all the reasons why I've never made my crush for the man known to him—or *anyone*, for that matter?

That all just leads me to another train of thought that's also known as the 'Crazy Train'. Because, surely I'd be a fool to think that we live in a world where my life with my demanding career, rebellious teenage daughter, and my whole world being here in Timber Falls, could ever intertwine with his busy, consuming, all family, all the time, rancher life at Eagle Mountain.

And even if we *did* pursue whatever this is, would anything that *could* happen between us ever have a chance? Ugh. This is too hard already.

"Everything OK there, Nora?" Randy asks, making me realize I've been staring at my cake rather than eating it.

It's then, when I see the gentle and inquisitive caring in his gaze, that I decide to take every argument I've had with myself about why this shouldn't or can't happen and throw it out the window.

"To answer your question, Randy. If you want to ask me out again, definitely do it as a 'date' date."

His brows jump up just as the corner of his mouth does the same. "And you'd accept?"

This time I decide I *can* make him squirm a little, because where's the fun in making things too easy for the man? "Well, you'll just have to wait until after dessert and try your luck, now, won't you?"

# 6

## RANDY

"Goddamnit!" I slam the phone down as I shoot out of my desk chair, the same old wooden and green leather one my father used before me that barely has any padding left. It rolls back and hits the overflowing bookcase–another piece of furniture leftover from my father's reign—causing a few loose pages to flutter to the ground. Now I'm pissed *and* I've made a mess.

Muttering to myself as I scoop them up and shove them back in place, I turn to the sound of footsteps and a soft wrap on my office door.

"Hey, Cass," I say to my cousin as I straighten up and re-tuck my shirt in at the belt. "What can I do for you?"

"We're about to check to see how many calves we can expect this season, so I was hoping to talk to you about moving the bulls. But after the way you slammed that phone down, I figure this is probably a crappy time, so I'll come back." I must be wearing my frustration all over my face, going by the wariness in his eyes, but since we all grew up together, my cousins know my moods blow through just as fast as they arrive.

"Every time is a crappy time when you have a stubborn rodeo manager up your ass."

Cass's brows jump up as he nods to the phone. "That's who you were talking to?"

"Yeah. And unsurprisingly, they won't back down over expecting their choice of bull calves in trade for giving us Big Bruiser. It's not somethin' that's gonna get resolved any time soon, so you may as well go over your concerns and plans with me now." I hold my hand out and gesture for him to give me the papers he's holding. It's suggestions for the manpower and production timelines, then the tools and equipment he requires for all the good work he does on the ranch. Cass's expertise is animal husbandry, so he monitors and oversees the breeding program for not only Eagle Mountain Ranch but also for almost every other ranch within the Eagle Mountain area. He also helps Kendra up at Horse Haven Sanctuary, so his time is just as in demand as mine—if not more so.

"They won't listen to reason?" he asks as he takes his seat across from mine. I rescue my chair from the bookcase, the rickety old wheels clanking against the wooden floor as I drag it in place.

"Logic and reality don't seem to be in their repertoire. We might end up needing legal support with this one. That's another headache I don't fuckin' need." I shake my head and I lean back into my chair with a sigh. "I honestly just need somethin' in my life to go easy for once. Ever since Dad passed, it's just been work, work, stress, and then more work. There doesn't seem to be any time for much else."

"You took on a lot when you stepped up to fill your father's shoes. And I think I speak for everyone in the family when I tell you how grateful we all are for everything you've done, Randy. This place is flourishin'. We all have security and abundance, and I don't think any of us could have done that without you leadin' the way."

"Appreciate that, Cass," I say, reaching out and handing him back the paper. "This is all fine, by the way. You can pull Miller and Beau off fence repairs to help you move the bulls. Colson too, if need be." Colson is Beau's brother-in-law and our youngest ranch hand at just nineteen. He's got a good head on his shoulders and has proven himself to be a valuable member of the ranch family.

"Thanks." He leans forward and takes his paperwork back from me. "If there's anything you need me to do—about the rodeo or around the ranch—you just let me know. I'm always here for you, cousin," he says genuinely.

"I know. And thank you, I appreciate that. I just wish this nonsense over the bull calves wasn't goin' on at all. We've got Jasper and Sarah's wedding to attend in a few weeks, and if this isn't sorted by then, it's gonna put a real dampener on the celebrations."

"Surely they'll call a cease-fire for the sake of their own daughter's wedding," Cass says as he stands to leave.

"Who the hell knows? All I know is that this is the first wedding the Call has resulted in that I'm dreading going to, and Jasper and Sarah deserve so much more than that from all of us. It's supposed to be a happy occasion, the bringin' together of two families, and Rod seems to think it should be all about him and what *he* wants. He's got it in his head that I should owe him this eternal debt of gratitude because both Josie and Sarah have left their family to join ours. And I just... I don't know how to respond to that. This isn't some reverse dowry situation from the dark ages. I just... I'm strugglin' to wrap my head around any of this."

"Sounds like you need a break away from it all."

"A break? With everythin' goin' on, that's the last thing on my To-Do List."

"OK. So you don't feel comfortable taking a break. But how about a proper night off? Ellie-Mae mentioned you were out on a date a couple of nights back. Is there any chance of a repeat with that one?"

A smile I wasn't expecting curves my mouth as I lose focus on my frustration and remember how beautiful Nora looked as she sat across the table from me. The vision is so clear that I swear I can still see her smile and hear her laugh, smell the sweet decadence of the warm chocolate brownies and melted ice cream in front of us. I can also feel the tingle against my palm from when I touched her hand...

"Holy shit," Cass says, snapping me out of my reverie. He chuckles, looking at me like I just let him read my diary. "So, Ellie *was* right. It wasn't a business dinner. And you, my man, are *smitten*."

I immediately clear my throat and shake my head. "Don't know what you're talkin' about. It was just a nice dinner."

"I've seen enough of y'all gettin' affected by this Call thing to be able to pick it by now."

"Yeah. Well, I don't think this is the Call. For starters, I've known this woman for years, so why didn't it happen sooner? And to finish, I'm not feelin' any of that *thump thump thump* thing that the others go on about. This is a simple case of man likes woman, woman likes man, and both of them dance around their feelings for a couple of years before going out on a business dinner that thankfully turned into a date dessert."

Cass laughs. "OK. Whatever you say, Randy. But since you have a 'man likes woman, woman likes man' situation going on, why don't you ask her to be your date for the weddin'? If she makes you go all doe-eyed like that just thinkin' about her, then she'll probably make an excellent distraction for your rodeo and bull calf problems too."

I raise my brow, considering his point because I have to admit, when I'm with Nora, I don't think about much else except the woman herself. I've spent the last few days trying desperately to figure out a smooth way to invite her out again, but would she be willing to attend a wedding as a second date? The only thing I can do is try my luck and ask...

# 7

## NORA

"Tip your hats and stomp your boots, everyone, as I introduce y'all to Mr. and Mrs. Jasper Barnes," Kendra announces as the officiant for the ceremony just before Jasper grabs his new wife, tips her backward, and proceeds to kiss the living daylights out of her. They go at it so passionately and for so long that my cheeks blush and I have to look away.

That's when I tip my gaze sideways to look at my handsome date for the occasion, my heart sighing when I see Randy's glassy eyes and happy smile. When I reach out to touch his arm, he looks down at me, wearing his emotions for all the world to see.

I grin at him. "They're beautiful."

"That they are," he replies gruffly, his eyes roaming my face. "So are *you*. I don't think I've made it clear just how stunnin' I think you look today, darlin'."

My lips curl up into a gentle smile, my own feelings bubbling up inside of me. "You flatter me."

He quirks a brow. "Ain't flattery if it's the truth, Nora." *The way he says my name does something to me... something I can't even explain.*

Needing a diversion to stop my brain from short-circuiting, I look around the gathering of guests, realizing we're getting left behind.

"We should probably go join the festivities."

"I *suppose* we should," I say, not moving, my smile widening in the same way Randy's does.

My gaze drops to his lips and suddenly it's like there's this pull drawing me closer to him, his doing the same.

"Randy!"

He jolts at the sound of the voice, as if coming out of a daze, and turns to where his brothers and cousins are standing in line to greet Jasper and Sarah. "I think I need to go offer my congratulations," he says, reaching an arm behind me to rest his hand on the small of my back over my peach floral dress. Even through the fabric, I can feel the heat of his skin leaving an imprint on mine, making me tremble.

"Yeah. Yeah, let's go." There's no missing the breathy tilt in my voice. I clear my throat, losing myself a little in the crinkling of his warm brown eyes. "I sure could do with a drink. The weather sure turned out nice, but it's hot standing out in the sun, isn't it?"

"It sure is." We walk down the aisle, and I step aside as Randy goes ahead to greet the happy couple, shaking Jasper's hand and giving Sarah a hug and kiss on the cheek alongside the rest of the family. Randy introduced me to everyone before the ceremony, and all of them were super-friendly and nice, Ellie-Mae particularly so, but I don't think marching up there and standing by his side in this moment is the right thing to do.

While that's happening, I take the time to look around the rodeo arena. We arrived a few hours before the ceremony and Randy showed me around the facilities, 'getting business out of the way so we can enjoy ourselves." The rodeo operation seems to be well run and from what Randy explained to me, they've been running for years, moving from town to town, using existing showgrounds, and setting up their own event within a day of arriving. All of their animals travel with them and they source any feed, hay and equipment they may need from local suppliers as they go before packing down and doing it all over again for the next event. From an outsider's perspective, it seems like they keep operating costs down with their biggest expense being the animals. This explains why the owners might be looking to utilize their new family connection with Eagle Mountain Ranch to their financial advantage. It makes good business sense, except for the part where it was never formally proposed to or agreed to by Randy or any of the Barnes family.

But after our tour, Randy made sure there was no misunderstanding about what today was. "Just to make it crystal clear, Nora," he said. "This *is* a date."

Suffice to say, that's something I'm *very* glad about.

I feel Randy's presence and turn around to meet him with a happy smile. His dark Stetson casts a sexy shadow over his face, his dress shirt, crisp blue Wranglers clinging to his bulky thighs. From the moment he picked me up this morning, I've been trying to decide whether I like this wedding look on him as much as his dessert date outfit a few weeks ago. What I *do* know is that so far, everything I've seen Randy wear looks damn good. *Then again, I've always thought that.*

"Hey."

"Hey, yourself."

"You ready to get this shindig started?" he asks.

"If you're asking if I'm ready for a drink, I am."

"Good to know," he says, sweeping his arm out toward the large white tents set up in the field outside the rodeo arena. "Shall we?"

I spot Jasper and Sarah escaping the arena, Jasper carrying her in his arms in the *opposite* direction to where the reception is being held, making me giggle.

"What's funny?"

I nod toward the runaway couple. "I'm thinking they're going to have a party of their own."

Randy chuckles and shakes his head. "Ah. Young love."

Quirking a brow, I look up at him. "How old is Jasper?"

"Thirty-two."

"And do you know how old I am, Randy Barnes?"

He looks nervous, his teeth worrying his bottom lip. "Not sure there's a right answer to that one and I ain't gonna guess and risk ruinin' our date."

*Ah, smart man.* I grin at him. "Well, *someone's* being a gentleman. But so you know, I'm thirty-one."

His eyes widen, but he wisely keeps his mouth shut. "Fuck. Now I'm even more in awe of you. Thirty-one and achieving everythin' you have? That's amazin'."

I feel my cheeks blush, my eyes drifting down to the dirt beneath my feet.

"Hey. No need to get bashful now. I believe I just complimented you."

I gently whack his arm. "You've called me amazing and beautiful. You're gonna give me a big head if you're not careful."

His answering grin fills me with a warmth that I'd bathe in forever given the chance. "Can't have *that* now, can we? Better go get you a drink before the swelling starts."

My brain *does* stutter this time, but I quickly recover. "Lead the way."

∽

AFTER DINNER HAS BEEN SERVED and eaten, and the wedding cake has been cut and hilariously smashed into Jasper and Sarah's mouths, all the tables and chairs are cleared away to the edge of the tent and an old man with a beard down to his stomach gets settled behind DJ turntables, announcing that the *real* party can now begin.

Randy and I are sitting on the edge of the makeshift dance floor, watching as his brothers and their wives kick up their boots to old-school country music.

"What's that grin for?"

"I was just thinking about how this is my first wedding."

His brows lift. "Ever?"

"Yep. And it's not even my own."

He studies me for what seems like a while. "Have you ever gotten close?"

"Wow," I say, feigning shock. "You're just going right on in there with the big questions today."

"Shit. Sorry. Forget I asked," he says, looking uncomfortable.

"Hey." I put my hand on his thigh and flex my fingers before pulling it back again, loving the flash of heat in his eyes that replaces his discomfort from before. "If we're dating, that's the kind of question you ask, right?"

He takes his hat off his head and rubs the back of his neck. "Not sure if you've noticed, but I'm a bit out of practice at this whole thing."

I gently bump my shoulder against his. "That makes the two of us."

"Really?"

"Uh *yeah*. I don't have time to do anything between work and home and my da... *mom*." He nods and I quickly get us back on track to avoid the weird feeling in my chest from not mentioning Leah. "But to answer your question, no. I've never gotten close to getting married."

"Good."

My brows shoot up. "Good?"

"Well obviously, if you were married, I wouldn't have such a beautiful woman on my arm as my weddin' date."

"And you say you're out of practice," I mutter, trying to ignore the heat in my cheeks.

"What was that?"

I wave him off with a giggle. "Nothing." Lifting my wineglass to my lips, I take a gulp, willing my heartbeat to slow down.

"Do you wanna get married?" he asks just as I'm about to swallow my mouthful, which means it all comes sputtering out of me.

"Right now?" I gasp, my voice sounding like a choking cat.

His smirk dazzles me. There's no other word to describe it. "Well, this *is* technically only our second date. I usually wait until at least date number five before pledging my troth to a woman I'm interested in."

"Interested in?" I ask, my heart racing in my chest–whether it's out of panic or excitement, I'm still not quite sure yet.

Randy's eyes turn heated as he very slowly looks me up and down, making me want to squirm in a good way. A *very* good way. "Definitely interested in you, Nora. Since we're here already, I might as well make my intentions *very* clear." He leans in close, so close that I feel his warm breath cascading over my suddenly sensitized skin, goosebumps covering my arms, and my heart beating a staccato symphony against my chest. "I want to spend time with you. I want to have more dates with you, no more family weddings or business meetings, just you and me getting to know each other. I want to meet your family and for you to get to know mine better." He reaches up and rests his palm on my cheek, a spark igniting between us when he touches me. His eyes widen before they fall hooded, so soft and warm and melty–just like my entire body right now. "I want to see where these feelings I have for you are going, Nora, and do somethin' for *me* for the first time in a long, long time. Whaddaya say?"

I lose myself in his gaze, fighting against every cell in my body, screaming at me to close the last of the distance between us and kiss this man who's been the star of all of my romantic dreams for the past few years now. But no way, no how will I do that at a family wedding in front of a bunch of strangers. Not with the way I want to kiss him right now.

Later though....

"I say..." I let my eyes drift over his handsome face, committing this moment to memory because never has a man been as honest and forthright about his intentions as he just was. "I say you should take me for a dance. What's a wedding without a little dancing with a handsome man?"

His smile is even more breathtaking than before as he stands and holds out his arm to me just as *The Way You Look Tonight* starts playing over the speakers. "Well, now. Will you let me have this dance?"

"Absolutely."

# 8

## RANDY

When the festivities are over and the newlyweds are off to their honeymoon cabin for a couple of weeks, the rest of us thank Rod and Phil for hosting us and make our way back to Eagle Mountain. While the agreement to keep talk of the bull calf dispute out of the celebrations held true for most of the day, Rod had had a few too many celebratory drinks by the end of the night and was beginning to forget his manners, so I was more than happy to say our goodbyes.

"Thanks for bringing me today," Nora says, smiling from where she's seated beside me, still holding onto the wedding bouquet she caught as we zoom down the darkened highway on our way back to Timber Falls. I thought it was mighty convenient that Sarah just happened to angle her body in a way that made sure the bouquet would fly my date's way, but I did appreciate the gesture. I think my brothers have been hoping for the Call to find its way to me as much as I have.

That's not to say that I think this *is* the Call—I think it's too early to determine that under the circumstances—but I wouldn't be unhappy if it turned out that Nora *was* my One. Doesn't explain why it took four years to happen, though...

"Thanks for accompanying me. I normally do this kind of thing stag, so the family was chuffed I brought someone along," I say, gesturing to the flowers in her lap.

"Oh, I noticed that too. But don't worry, I'm not clinging to this like it's a sign we're going to get married or anything. I know I got confused earlier when I thought you were saying we should get married right away, but you have to know that I would have said no even if you were serious. My life…it's too complicated for me to go rushing into anything. I hope I'm making sense and not coming off sounding ungrateful or like I don't want a relationship with you to happen—because I do—I just need things to happen slowly. Is that OK?"

She sucks in a lungful of air after saying all of that in a rush, and I glance away from the road for a moment to offer her an understanding smile. Because suddenly, the likelihood of this actually being the Call seems a little more plausible—depending on what this complication of hers is, of course.

"Of course it's OK. I meant what I said back there. I want to see where this attraction between us goes, and I'm willin' to keep waitin' and movin' things forward on your terms. I both like and respect you, Nora. There ain't a single part of me that would want you to ever feel pressured or uncomfortable in any way."

"I don't think I could ever feel uncomfortable around you, Randy. To be honest, you're the first man I've even *entertained* dating in a very long time. This...complication—I really don't like using that word for it, but it'll have to do for now—it's made me very wary about who I get close to. There's just a lot going on behind the scenes for me."

"OK. I'm hearin' you, and I'm also hearin' that you aren't ready to go into detail just yet, so I'll respect your privacy and let you open up to me when you feel safe and ready to do so."

"God, you're a catch, Randy Barnes. Most men would take this conversation as an instant rejection."

"Well, if that's how they react, then I wouldn't go callin' them men. I'd call them impatient boys who weren't datin' you for the right reasons."

"And you are?"

I glance at her again, and she's leaning against the headrest, smiling broadly at me. "Yes, ma'am. My intentions are as pure as they come."

"Oh, yeah?" she says, arching a brow. "Well, if you don't mind, I'd like to test the purity of those intentions of yours."

A grin pulls up the side of my mouth. "Is that so?"

"If you take the next right and drive slowly, you'll find the lookout we used to park at when we were randy teenagers. Pun not intended."

"Ha. I'd like to say I never heard that joke before but..."

"Not so original, huh?" She laughs and leans back to toss the bouquet of flowers into the backseat as I turn off the main road. "Well, at least the view's about to get good for you. From up here, you can see the entire valley below, and it's real pretty at this time of night."

"It's already pretty. So damn pretty you've been making this ol' rancher look a hell of a lot better all day," I say, driving slowly until I arrive in a secluded parking area that already contains a couple more cars.

"You make me blush, Randy."

"I could do and say a hell of a lot more to make you blush, but this is a test of my resolve, right? Park at the local make-out spot and just enjoy the sights? I'm in my forties, sweetheart. I thought I had control over my randiness, but you keep challenging my restraint." I turn to her and wink as I shut off the engine and look out at the glittering town below.

"I didn't just bring you here for the view, Randy." She turns to me and unclips her seatbelt. "I brought you here to make out."

"In that case," I say, reaching under my seat and sliding it backward to give her space as she climbs onto my lap. "I'll let my randiness come out to play a little."

With a giggle, she settles over me, sweeping her hair over one of her shoulders as she rakes her painted nails through my beard. "Just a little. We're taking this slow, remember?"

"Oh, I remember," I say, my hands moving to her hips as I lift my face to hers, our lips brushing as my voice lowers to a whisper. "Although, I can't be held accountable for the way my body responds to having a beautiful, sexy woman in my lap. It's been a while, and you're fuckin' gorgeous."

"Now I'm really blushing," she murmurs, just before our mouths connect.

My hand goes straight to the back of her head, the gentle beginnings of the kiss quickly getting more intense and heated as our tongues probe and taste.

"I've gotta say, I wasn't expecting tonight to go this way," I say, pulling back slightly as Nora looks at me with hooded eyes.

"And here was me really hoping it would," she says, grinning before we meet in the middle again, our tongues barely meeting before a loud, 'What the fuck?' cuts through the moment and we quickly pull apart.

"Oh my god," Nora gasps, scrambling off my lap and back to her seat as I wind my window down slightly to ask our interrupter what their problem is.

"Is there something wrong, miss?" I ask of the heavily eye-shadowed teenager with the long, dark, messy hair and a scowl that'd scare even the hardest of men.

"Yeah, dude. There's a whole lot wrong. What the hell are you doing kissing my mom?"

"Your... what?" I blink rapidly as I look from the girl to Nora, then back and forth again.

Nora's gaze shifts from our interrupter to lock with mine, a multitude of emotions flitting through her eyes, her mouth pressing into a thin line. "Randy Barnes, meet Leah. My daughter."

# 9

## NORA

I don't give myself time to study Randy's reaction to my *complication*. Instead, I quickly swing the door open, jumping down and shutting Randy in before I can give too much thought to what this may or might mean for *whatever* it is between us.

Because my number one priority right now is finding out why my daughter–my *sixteen-year-old* daughter–is gallivanting around the town when she's *supposed* to be at home.

Rounding the hood of Randy's truck, I'm just about to open my mouth to let rip at Leah when she beats me to the punch.

"So *this* is where you disappeared to today? Off to suck face with whoever *this* is, hey Nora?"

"Leah, please lower your voice and watch your tone," I say, trying to get my wits about me in the face of a clearly brazen and overconfident sixteen-year-old, especially given the tall, lanky, pierced, and purple-haired boy standing behind her with a knowing smirk on his face and a...OMG is that a hickey on his neck? *My daughter is a vampire.* Somehow I register Randy getting out and standing behind me, but I don't dare look at him.

"Oh, no, Mommy dearest. You totally lost the high road when I caught you with your tongue down this man's throat. Eww, by the way." She grimaces overdramatically, but then grins gleefully over my shoulder. "Although, nice catch there, Nora."

"Leah McIntyre. Stop showing off and deflecting. You're supposed to be at home studying for your final on Monday."

She rolls her eyes and waves her hand in the air. "I'm gonna fail, anyway. So I decided it was pointless to try and study. Life's too short, and Heath here was asking me to come out."

My mouth drops open as the kid with her–and he may be taller than me but he's totally a kid–reaches out and grabs my daughter's ass like he owns it, and I could've sworn I heard a muted growl behind my back coming from Randy too.

"C'mon, L. Let's go."

She turns and beams up at the boy-child-goth-rocker wannabe. Inwardly I wince because I *also* fell for the dyed-hair, eyeliner-wearing bad boy at fifteen, and I'm looking at the result of that standing right in front of me!

"What about Nanny? Does *she* know where you are?'

That's when I see it, that flash of my good girl who I hold out hope will win out over whatever *this* version of my loving daughter is. "She fell asleep in front of the TV after I told her I was going to bed. She doesn't know I'm not home."

I pop a hip and glare at her, giving her the mom look to end all mom looks. "You don't think she might be *worried* when she wakes up and goes to check on you?"

"I was gonna be home by then, anyway. Well, until I decided to mess with couples at Makeout Point and almost barfed when I saw it was my own *mom*." The goth boy-child laughs and starts to make gagging noises, earning another smirk from Leah.

"You're coming with me right now and we're going home."

She shakes her head. "Nuh-uh, Nora. Not tonight. I'll go home now, but I ain't going in that passion wagon. Eww."

"Leah," I growl, my grip on my anger slipping away.

She waves me off like what I said doesn't even matter. "I'll leave you to it. Hey, Ma. Who knows? Maybe this one won't dump you with a kid like the last one did, huh?" Then I watch in stunned silence as my once angelic, doting daughter hooks her arm with her pierced, purple spikey-haired companion and storms off like a queen lauding over her kingdom like she doesn't have a care in the world or is worried about any consequences that are damn well coming her way.

Feeling Randy's heat at my back, I close my eyes and take a slow deep breath, willing myself to calm down and not do what I really want to do right now which is chase after my daughter, hog-tie her, drive her back home and lock her in her room for say the next ten years.

*Unfortunately, that kind of behavior is frowned upon.*

"I'm sorry, Randy. I guess the cat—or the *brat*—is out of the bag, so to speak," I say quietly, not yet brave enough to turn around and see the expected disappointment written all over the man's face. *God. What must he think of me right now?*

Big hands frame my hips from behind. Then I'm slowly being tugged toward him, my back meeting his wide chest just as his arms wrap around my waist and cross over front. I let my head lean into the side of his, a shiver coursing through me when his lips brush soothingly over the crook of my neck. "Seems we've got a bit of catchin' up to do when it comes to your daughter."

My body stiffens, but Randy acts quickly, smoothing his hands up and down my middle like I'm a skittish mare, ready to bolt. "Hey. Deep breaths. Whatever is going on between you two, it'll get better."

"Well, it can't exactly get any *worse* now, can it? I just had it out with my sixteen-year-old daughter that the hot rancher I'm crushing on had no idea even existed until now. *And* that was after said daughter interrupted what was the hottest make-out session of my life."

He chuckles–*chuckles*–before turning me around and backing me against the side of his truck, not stopping until his body is cloaking mine. *Rusty, my ass.* "Well"—he smiles--" breaking this down, your complication is not a mystery to me anymore." His expression falls and his intense gaze burns through me. "But why you thought she'd be a complication to whatever this is between us, *is* a question you need to ask yourself." He runs his hands up my sides until he cups my neck, pinning me in place. "Because there isn't one thing about you,

Nora McIntyre, that I don't want to know about. And however long it takes me to prove that to you, I'll do it."

My eyes fill with tears. How can this man be so. damn. perfect in every way? Like surely he'd run for the hills-or back to his ranch at least– when faced with a showdown between his thirty-one-year-old accountant/date and her surly, rebellious, mouthy teenage daughter who'd just interrupted the end of his date. A date where we may have agreed to take things slowly, but there was nothing slow and not hot about all of that kissing and rutting against each other. *It was the most fun I haven't had by myself in forever.*

"You're not mad?"

Randy leans in and brushes his mouth against mine, leaving my lips tingling in his wake. "Curious? Intrigued? Want to know more about you and Leah and how that all came to be? Absolutely. Mad? Fuck no." Then he kisses me again, not hot and heavy, but slow and steady, almost methodical in his intent to relax and reassure me. When he finally pulls away again, he rests his forehead to mine as we catch our breath, which isn't an easy thing to do since every single nerve ending in my body has been sparked to life and is demanding more from Randy and his talented mouth...and lips... and tongue.

"What happens now?" I ask, breathlessly.

"Well, as much as I wanna stay here with you doing this and other stuff, I think I should get you home so you can prepare yourself for the next showdown with your daughter."

"You're a smart man, Randy Barnes."

He snorts. "I've just lived through my brothers and cousins gettin' into more than enough trouble for the whole district and then some growin' up. So I know that this was just round one."

"More like round one hundred and twenty-five of many," I mutter as I just stand there and hug him, hoping to absorb some of his strength and steadiness.

"And there'll be many more, but there's a difference now, Nora." He smooths his hands up and down my arms. "You wanna know what that is?"

I scrunch my brows and tilt my head, not exactly sure what he could mean. "What?"

"You've got me to lean on, now. 'Cause if you think this has put me off, think again. If anything, I'm more hooked on you now than I was the minute you climbed into my lap." He dips his face to mine. "And I was already a goner well before that, darlin'." He grins at the catch in my breath. "But time to get you home. We can continue the interrupted make-out session at our *next* date this week."

I jerk back, still stunned that Randy Barnes is not running for the hills–or the mountain–and far, far away from me and my teenager drama. "Another date? Already?"

He pecks the tip of my nose. "Gotta get to date number five somehow."

## 10

## RANDY

"Wanna tell me how your date went?" Cass says as we move through the field of cows, the doppler in hand as he checks each one for signs of pregnancy. We used to do this the old-fashioned way—rectally—but with modern advancements, we can get this done faster and less invasive than in the past.

"You were there for most of it. We ate, drank and danced. She caught the bouquet, then I drove her home to Timber Falls."

"She lives in Timber Falls?" Cass asks.

"Yeah, right near her accountancy firm. She's got a place out there with her mom. I'm heading out that way to take her out again tomorrow night," I respond.

Cass glances over and chuckles softly. "Would I be right in assumin' you're a bit smitten with this lady, Randy Barnes?"

"Smitten? I don't know. But I definitely like her a hell of a lot."

He quirks a brow. "Reckon it might be the Call comin' your way?"

"You know, I've thought about that myself, but I just can't be sure. Seems kinda strange that it just magically happens when I've finally gotten jack of waitin' and decided to take matters into my own hands."

"That's true. You know, sometimes I've wondered if it's the mere *suggestion* of the Call that's makin' everyone so sure they're hearin' it. Like, maybe believin' there's a mystical Mountain Spirit who chooses your soulmate for you makes it easier to fall in love without throwing up all the normal roadblocks most folks like to complicate things with. Maybe that feelin' of sureness makes all the difference?"

"Maybe," I say, holding the doppler while he makes some notes in his logbook. "How they lookin' so far?"

"Most are measurin' around eight weeks. So we're doing well right now."

We continue moving through the herd, checking each animal for pregnancy. By the end, we're both pretty certain there won't be any more additions to this particular herd until next year. We've already got them bred for later in the season, but just to keep things tidy, Cass and I agree to go through and check how many heifers are pregnant before we call it a day.

"So you gonna tell me more about your Nora? You kinda kept her to yourself most of the wedding."

"You blame me?"

"She's beautiful, that's for sure. So, no, don't blame 'ya there. I'd probably do the same in your shoes."

"And she's not just beautiful. She's smart too. One of the smartest I know."

"High praise comin' from you."

"She's the reason this ranch is doin' as well as it is. Most of those ideas for diversifyin'—like us buyin' up the supply store—were all her idea. All it took was me tellin' her my vision for the future and she just worked to make it bigger and better."

"Sounds like a great person to have in your corner."

"Yeah. It's part of why I really want to be in hers, too. She's got a teenage daughter who seems to be rebellin' a bit right now, so I want her to feel like she can come to me with her troubles, the way I've been goin' to her."

"A teenage daughter? She seems young to have a kid at all, let alone a teen."

"I don't know the story behind it, but doin' the math, she would have been fifteen/sixteen herself when Leah was born."

Cass nods his head as if considering something. "I'm sure she'll tell you everythin' in time. Do you care that she's got a kid?"

"Not at all. You know I love kids, so datin' someone with a fully grown one doesn't faze me. I just don't wanna see her struggle."

"I hear you on that, cousin. No one wants to see someone they care about goin' through a hard time. But if I know you, you'll be right there easin' her burden. Same as you've done for all of us time and time again."

"That's what family does," I say with a nod.

"Yeah. But with the way you've stepped in to help Remy whenever he flies off the rails, you have to know it's more than appreciated. We all owe you a debt of gratitude."

"Don't mention it. Although, if you wanna put some of that gratitude to the test, you can always come out here and help me feed. It seems like Beau has been sendin' young Colton out to do all the feed runs lately, but it's a big job and not somethin' Colton should be doin' on his own."

"Of course," Cass says. "But maybe Beau is tryna teach the kid how to fail a little, so he learns how to handle stuff on his own."

I nod thoughtfully for a moment before responding. "Maybe that's true, but there's enough of us out here that no man needs to be hauling all that feed on his own. If it isn't you helpin', then maybe Finn or Jasper can help."

"I'll get it sorted, Randy. Promise."

"Great," I say, stepping away as my cell starts to vibrate in my pocket. When I pull it out and see Nora's name light up on the screen, I let Cass know it's important and make my way out of the field and onto the other side of the fence.

"Hey, darlin'," I say into the receiver after I call her back. "Sorry I missed you. I was in with the cows and—"

"It's fine. I was just calling because..."

"What is it, Nora? You sound a bit off."

Heavy breaths can be heard on my side of the line. "It's just...I hate having to call you and ask for help but, it's Leah. She's gotten into some trouble and she's currently at the police station."

"In Timber Falls?" I'm already walking back toward the ranch house to get my keys for my truck.

"No. Anchorage."

I stop dead in my tracks. "Anchorage? How the heck did she get all the way there?"

"She and her friend hopped on a train without a ticket. They got picked up by inspectors at the other end and... Gosh, I'm just too worked up and I need someone to drive me."

"I'll be at your place in an hour."

"Are you sure?"

"Of course, darlin. Anything you need, I'm here, OK?"

The sigh of relief is all my heart needs to know that I'm making the right decision. "Thank you, Randy. This means so much."

"I'll see you soon."

I hang up the phone and start sprinting toward the house, not even bothering to change out of my work clothes. I know Nora must be a wreck if she's called me for help, and I'm more than happy to answer *that* call. I hate to say it, but sometimes getting picked up by the cops is just what a kid needs to straighten themselves out. With any luck, Leah might learn her lesson and come back home with a new appreciation for the family that loves her. Crossing my fingers that everything turns out all right, I jump in my truck and hit the open road.

## 11

## NORA

"I'm so sorry. I know you must have enough on your plate already without *me* piling more trouble onto it," I say from the passenger seat of Randy's truck as we make our way along the highway from Timber Falls and toward Anchorage.

"Darlin', I'm glad you called me. I wanna be that person for you." I stamp down the need to kiss him senseless for proving once again that he's such a good man. But since we're driving and I don't wanna distract him, I have to settle with reaching over and giving his hand a squeeze to convey my gratitude.

I turn to look out the window while my head and heart struggle with being worried sick about my wayward daughter and being absolutely livid that she'd put herself in potential danger like that. I mean, she stowed away on a *train* to *Anchorage,* of all places.

When I got the call telling me she was being held by the police in Anchorage until a parent or guardian could come to collect her, I immediately freaked out and was halfway out the door when Mom stopped me and suggested I call a friend to drive me. Randy was the first person to pop into my mind. And like the wonderful man I've always known him to be, he didn't hesitate to offer his help, assuring me we'd drive straight through to get to Leah as quickly as possible.

Turning his hand over and lacing his fingers with mine, he gives me a gentle squeeze. "Since we've got hours of driving ahead of us, how about we talk about you and your not so little *complication*, huh?"

Strangely, that brings a small smile to my lips as I look over and meet his side glance. "OK. What do you wanna know?"

"Everythin', Nora. If it's about you, I want to hear it all." I swear my heart just swooned and sighed all at once, if that is even physically possible. Whatever it is, the way Randy makes me feel whenever I'm near him is becoming addictive.

I laugh quietly and shake my head, my cheeks heating a little. "I'm not all that interesting."

Randy lifts my hand and brushes his lips over my knuckles, never once taking his eyes off the highway. "Now *that* I don't believe for a minute."

"You might change your mind once I get started," I tease with a smile before I sit back and let out a sigh. "OK. So I guess we should start with Leah, then?"

He nods, but even lowering our arms back to the seat between us, he doesn't let go. It's like he needs the physical connection with me as much as I need it with him. Knowing that is a little heady, to say the least.

"It's a pretty cliche story that might sound a little familiar. A rebellious latch-key teenager with a hard-working single mom falls in with the wrong crowd, falls for the wrong boy, and bada bing, bada boom, she gets pregnant and that boy wants absolutely nothing to do with it. He didn't want to be a dad, *or* accept the consequences of the baby he helped make." Randy's fingers flex in mine before releasing instantly, my eyes darting up to see a muscle twitching in his jaw, his gaze hard and pinned straight ahead.

"He wanted *nothing* to do with either of you?"

"Nuh-uh, and honestly, that's a good thing, because when I say he was the wrong boy, that's not an understatement. Right after Leah was born, he was caught up in a burglary ring that ended up seriously hurting a shopkeeper. So he went down for felony grievous bodily harm, and I've never heard a single thing about him since."

"What does Leah think about that?"

"She knows what happened. It's not something I've ever kept from her. But he's not listed on the birth certificate and his parents never reached out or anything... So, Mom and I have just tried to be everything she'd ever need. And yes that has meant sacrificing any chance of having a private life, but doing it for my daughter so she doesn't end up making the same errors in judgment I made when I was young, and knowing that if she needs us, Mom and I are there for her, it's made it worth it. Well, I think so anyway."

"I knew that about you as soon as I met you."

My brows scrunch together. "What's that?"

"That you're the type of person who'd go above and beyond for anyone, but especially those you care about." *God! This man!*

"I could say the same thing about you, Randy Barnes. You're all about your family and that ranch."

His lips curve up, and he catches my eyes for a moment. "Now I hope you know I'm adding my beautiful, smart, *sexy* accountant to that list."

My replying smirk mimics his. "Oh, so I'm just an accountant, am I?"

"Ah. Um... no. I added the word sexy to that, but...shit..." I shouldn't find it so adorable to have this big burly rancher stumbling over his words, but I quickly put him out of his misery.

"Relax, Randy. I was just teasing you. But I would like to think we're a little bit more than accountant and client now."

"Fuck yes we are. And if we weren't racin' the clock to pick up your daughter, I'd be pullin' this truck over and showin' you *just* how much more."

"Maybe we should take a rain check on that show and tell?"

"Maybe we should. But for the record, it'll be *all* show and *no* tell." His smirk turns devilishly sexy this time. "Mainly 'cause the show will do *all* the telling required."

*Damn, is it hot in here?*

"Right, how about we change the subject before you have me self-combusting right here in your truck?" And that's the honest to god truth, because the more I think about *Randy's* version of show and tell, the more I realize it's been a long, long time since I've even thought of a man this way, and the more I want to be shown... *everything he has to offer.*

"Well, we definitely can't have that now, can we?" he says with a chuckle. "Then *I'd* have to try and deal with your daughter alone, and I'd be the first to say that I may have lived through my brothers and cousins bein' a handful, and even Ellie-Mae too, but somethin' tells me Leah might be a *whole* other kettle of fish."

I giggle because from what I've seen of his family, and what I *know* of Leah's behavior in the past six months, he's probably not wrong about that. "She's gone from sweet to sassy to total delinquent faster than I thought possible, that's for sure."

"Do you know what might've caused it?"

"My guess is she's following in her mother's footsteps and running wild for the sake of a boy. And I have a feeling her catching us in a lip lock the other day didn't really help matters."

"You want me to make myself scarce when you head into the police station, then? I don't wanna cause trouble."

"Oh no. I don't want that at all. I've always been honest with Leah, and I don't want to start hiding things from her now."

"That's probably wise."

I bounce a shoulder. "Who really knows what's right or wrong with raising kids these days? We're all just feeling our way around the dark, but we do our best and hope that's enough. Both Mom and I have always been very present while Leah was growing up. If I couldn't be there due to studying or work, or setting up my own business, Mom was always there. It's one of the many reasons why we bought our house together."

"It's amazin', that's what that is."

I look down at our still joined hands, swallowing down the lump of emotion in my throat. "Thank you. But it was honestly a lifesaver for all of us. Mom's had a few minor health scares over the years, and with my busy schedule as well as juggling a rather rambunctious and highly intelligent daughter, all of us living together has been a godsend. I don't know what I would've done without Mom at my back."

"It's what family does."

I nod because he's not wrong. "So all we've done is made sure Leah knows what's expected of her and what the boundaries are, but also making sure that she knows we love her, we're both there for her, and our doors are always open if she wants to talk to us about anything. And at first, it was just little things like answering back to me and a bit of attitude. Mom even told me it was like watching history repeating itself, and it was payback for me being a handful as a teen. But now I know she's just as worried as I am because it's like we catch glimpses of the sweet, caring, responsible young woman we both know she is, but the times we're seeing that side of her are getting few and far between."

"It doesn't surprise me one bit that you're a good mom, Nora. I can't imagine you bein' anything *but*."

"A good mom who didn't know her daughter jumped on the train across the state to Anchorage without a damn ticket. How's that being a good mom?"

"The fact you care enough to get your ass out there to help her is what makes you *great*."

"I honestly don't feel great at anything right now."

"I hear you. During tough times, it seems the only thing we can see in ourselves is our faults and the faults of those around us. But if she's as smart as you, it makes sense she'd get one past you. And to be fair, that's a pretty elaborate adventure she tried to go on. Any idea what her plan was?"

"Nope. All I know is that she and her friend—Heath—thought a trip to Anchorage was a *great* idea, but they got caught when it came to showing their tickets."

"So we're pickin' them both up?"

"Hell no. I think Heath needs some time to think about leading my girl astray," I say with a smirk because it may be harsh, but I'm also aware he has a rescue squad coming his way too. "And he has his own parents. His father happens to be an old client of mine–and a lawyer, to boot. David and Abigail are also currently driving to Anchorage, except they told me in no uncertain terms that they plan on taking their time so that their son can 'think about his actions'." Randy chuckles and shakes his head at my low, deep imitation of the father's words.

"OK, then. Sounds like y'all have this under control." A silent beat goes by before he glances at me again, a question in his eyes. "So you, your Mom, and Leah. Has it always just been the three of you?"

Detecting the tight, maybe curious tone in Randy's voice, I tilt my head and study the man who's been the main star of my thoughts and feelings.... and other things... ever since the Makeout Point kiss.

"Is that your way of asking me if there's been any serious relationships in my past, Randy?"

"Hmm. Maybe."

"Well, I'm telling you right now, the answer is no. I've been all about work and my daughter. That's until a certain rancher walked into my office a few years ago asking for my help."

I watch with delight as his eyes widen and his lips tilt in a sexy smirk.

"Well damn, darlin'. That's about the best thing anyone's ever said to me. You've just about stolen the words right out of me."

I look down at the GPS monitor on the dashboard of his truck. "Lucky we've got a few more hours of driving for you to reclaim them again," I say with a beaming smile, earning a rumbled growl under his breath and a heated gaze.

"Once all this is sorted and your Leah is back home with you tucked up safe, you and me are arrangin' another date, Nora McIntyre. I want you to come out to the ranch and I'll cook you dinner. Just the two of us."

"A sleepover date?" I ask, biting my lip to stifle my excited giggles. This thing between us is moving at warp speed, but damn, I like how it feels.

He glances my way with yet another surprised smirk. "I was gonna be a gentleman and let the wind decide that for us, but yeah, I'd really like to have a sleepover date with you, Nora. Not that there'll be a hell of a lot of sleepin' going on, but I can promise there'll be a whole lot of explorin'."

I press my knees together at the thought. "Looking forward to it, rancher."

Randy adjusts himself in his seat with a grunt. "Me too, darlin'."

Hours later, we arrive in Anchorage, and after finding the police station, any flirtatiousness between Randy and me flies out the proverbial window. All fun chatting and banter is replaced by dealing with–well, being ignored by–my surly and yet very quiet sixteen-year-old daughter who'd rather shoot daggers at us with her eyes and text incessantly on her phone than spare a moment to talk to us or respond to any of my many questions. Just an hour into the drive back home, I'm almost relieved when Randy pulls into the parking lot of a nice-looking motel that's just off the highway near a small blink-and-you-miss-it town called Spring Haven.

Turning off the engine, he twists in his seat to look between the two of us McIntyre women–one scowling, one wishing she had a manual on how to raise a teenage girl who seems hellbent on following the path I paved with my own teenage belligerence. Why can't kids just *listen* and *learn* from the mistakes their parents make? It's like the only way they figure anything out is to experience it first-hand. It feels impossible to stop, and even harder to watch.

"I'm not stayin' in this dump," Leah gripes immediately.

"Well, that decision ain't up to you," Randy rumbles in his slow yet calm way. "I'm makin' the executive decision that we're gonna bed down here for the night." Leah's brows immediately shoot up. "Separate rooms, of course. You and your mom in one. Me by myself in another. So you can get whatever that thought is right out of your head." His lips twitch as Leah rolls her eyes and scoffs. And it's in that moment I realize that he's all onboard this wrangling-a-surly-teen adventure right alongside me. *And god am I thankful for that!*

"Whatever," Leah says. "Beats sitting in the back of this stinky truck for another five hours. What do you put in here? Pig shit?"

"Leah!" I scold, but Randy just laughs my daughter's rudeness off.

"What you're smellin' is hard work and the scent of all the Mountain Spirit provides, Leah. You should come out to the ranch sometime and experience it for yourself. Beats ridin' trains without a ticket, and there's a heck of a lot more fun and danger involved."

"Unlikely," Leah says, folding her arms tighter across her chest.

Randy chuckles as he climbs out of the truck and turns back to us. "Now you two stay here and I'll go get us our rooms."

"Thanks, Randy," I say, shooting him what I hope is a reassuring smile. "For everything." That earns me a wink and a tip of his hat before he turns and strides into the motel reception.

As I watch him go, all I can think is that I must've done something right in my life to deserve a man like him in my corner. Randy Barnes is one of a kind, and I can't wait until the time when life for both of us settles down and we have the chance to explore this growing thing between us–especially that sleepover he promised. When all this is over, I'm definitely looking forward to *that*.

## 12

## RANDY

After a somewhat frustrating night's sleep, I lean against the hood of my truck while waiting for Nora and Leah. It was hard knowing that Nora was so near to me all night, but being unable to go to her and offer comfort during what I know is a difficult time. I have and still do deal with the stress of wayward family members, but I imagine that feeling of powerless frustration is tenfold when it's your own child. Being the fixer I am, I want to do something to make this easier for both Nora and Leah, but I haven't quite figured out how to broach the situation, or even if my solutions would be welcomed the way they are back on the ranch.

When I look up, the two women are crossing the parking lot toward me, still wearing the clothes they had on yesterday. Leah is fresh-faced and has her jacket tied about her waist and both women have their hair scraped up into ponytails. I can see the family resemblance now that the emo eye makeup is gone. The girl definitely takes after her mom. They even walk the same way.

"Mornin' ladies," I call out, loving the way Nora's tight features soften the moment she meets my eyes. "You sleep OK?"

"As well as can be expected," Nora sighs as they come to a stop in front of me, and her whole face brightens with a smile. It has me thinking back to all the times we've had meetings and that same sparkle would be in her gaze. At the time, I thought it was for the love of her work. But now I'm wondering how much of a jackass I've been for not paying her the proper attention and waiting so damn long to act on these feelings of mine. *Not gonna be wastin' any more time now, that's for sure.*

"As long as you got *some* rest," I say, stepping forward and kissing Nora's cheek chastely before moving back. I turn to her daughter and smile. "Mornin' Leah." She lifts her chin and grunts a little in response. I'm calling that progress. "Was thinkin' we'd grab some breakfast. There's a diner a few minutes down the road that's not too bad."

"Sounds great to me," Nora says. "What do you think, sweetheart? Pancakes or maybe waffles for breakfast?" Nora turns to Leah with a smile and gets a half-hearted shrug in response. *Well, that's not a no...*

"Let's go then," I say, looking between the two women. "I have a hankerin' for some of their famous corned beef hash and eggs. Doesn't hold a candle to my sister, Ellie-Mae's, cookin' but it's good grub all the same. We can walk there." I incline my head in the direction of the diner and set off with both quickly following. Nora closes the distance between us and surprises me by reaching out for my hand. Not that I'm complaining, but the fact she's demonstrative in front of Leah says a lot.

"I think I might get the corned beef hash too," she says, glancing up at me as I lace my fingers with hers.

"How about you, Leah? What are you hankerin' for?" I ask.

"Coffee," she grunts before pushing off on her boot heel to walk ahead of us before taking a left turn out of the parking lot.

"When should we tell her she's going in the wrong way?" I say to Nora as the teen girl stomps off.

"Give her a minute." Nora giggles, her soulful eyes dancing when they meet mine. "She'll figure it out soon enough."

"You OK?" I ask while I have her alone.

"Yeah. She fell asleep as soon as her head hit the pillow. After I called and updated Mom, I just lay there awake, staring at the ceiling and questioning every decision I've ever made throughout my entire life. How about you?"

"Well, I'd have felt a hell of a lot better with you in my arms, but there'll be a time and a place for those things."

An agreeable sigh escapes her. "Believe me, there's nowhere I would've preferred to be. Well, maybe a bit closer to home than halfway across the state, but yeah... The feeling's mutual, Randy."

There's no hiding how great it feels to know the person you want also wants you in return, so I shoot her a huge grin. Which also happens to coincide with me catching sight of Leah jogging our way, having finally realized she was stomping off in the wrong direction.

"What're you grinning so wide about Randy Barnes?" Nora asks with a coy smile.

"Firstly, I'm just happy being here with you. And secondly, we've got company." I shift my gaze to where Leah is now stomping along behind us, her arms folded tight across her chest and a scowl on her face.

"Nice of you to join us," Nora throws over her shoulder.

"You could've told me I was following the wrong path," Leah snaps, which only causes Nora to take a lung-filling breath and shoot her a knowing smile.

"Oh my sweet girl, I've been telling you that for months now. You're just not listening."

Leah's eyes flash bright green in response, but she doesn't offer a retort, only a scowl and a look of deep concentration that gives me hope that there's still time to reach her before she goes fully off the rails. And with my experience wrangling every Barnes brother, cousin or acquaintance with a chip on their shoulder, coupled with Nora's unwillingness to give up on her daughter, I'm sure that *together* we can turn this all around.

## 13

## NORA

I make sure I leave the office at five on the dot on Monday night. Mom, Leah and I have dinner plans together. Nothing fancy, just a gathering of family around the kitchen table, but I think it's important because even though Leah has been grounded for two weeks and has lost her phone and internet privileges to boot, she still needs to experience happy moments and togetherness so she can see that Mom and I are not her enemies. We're here to help and guide her, and while I get the need to act out and express yourself, there are ways to do that other than criminal acts that take you hours away from home and safety.

"Anything I can help with?" I ask as I enter the kitchen, the scent of butter, pork, and herbs guiding the way from the moment I entered the front door. I set my bag and coat over the back of a chair and make my way over to my mother, who's busy over the stove.

"You can put your bag and coat away," Mom says, giving me a sly grin as I drop a kiss on the top of her head. I'm a good foot taller than her, but she's still as big in personality to me as she always was.

"I'll do it when I go upstairs to change," I say, grabbing a green bean and crunching down on it as I lean my hips against the counter next to her. "How was everything today?"

"Strained. She's spent most of the day in her room blasting music in her ears. It's like déjà vu." Her raised brow makes a pit form in my stomach, because now that I'm on the other side of it, I hate that I ever made her feel this way while I was growing up. All day, all I've been thinking about is what *could* have happened. What if she got hurt, or lost, or something? What if Heath and she had gotten separated, and she was all alone? Just the thought of that has me shuddering and fighting back tears. So now, more than ever, I feel awful about the anguish I caused my mom growing up.

"I'm so sorry I ever did this to you, Mom."

"Oh, I'm sure I gave my own mother something to grow ulcers over myself. Seems it's a rite of passage for the McIntyre girls. But I think we all turned out OK, don't you?" She lifts a hand and pats me lightly on the cheek. "If I don't say it enough, I am really proud of the woman you've become. And I'm certain you'll be feeling the same way about Leah in about twenty years. She's just...learning who she is."

"Shame she's so hell-bent on doing it the hard way," I say, stealing another bean and pushing off the counter. "I'm gonna head up and grab a quick shower and change into some comfy clothes. How long do I have?"

"About ten minutes," she says, smiling up at me before I give her a quick hug then grab my stuff and make my way upstairs. I'm so grateful to have Mom here to help guide me through this difficult stage of motherhood. We've transitioned over the years from being adversaries to best friends, so I'm holding on to the hope that one day, that will be Leah and me, too.

Pausing just outside Leah's door, I push it open slightly and spot her sitting on her bed with a set of red headphones on and a book propped open against her knees. She spots me immediately.

"Spying on me now?" she asks suspiciously, pushing one side of her headphones behind her ear.

I smile serenely, not wanting to pay her comment with any sort of conflict. "Just popping in to say hi. You have a good day?"

"Not really," she grumbles.

"Good book?"

She lifts the copy of Author Seeking Mountain Man off her lap and shrugs. "It's a little wishy-washy, but I like that I know the place the author is writing about."

"Maybe we can take a trip out there one day? Do a little mountain man sight-seeing adventure."

"Maybe," she says with another shrug. "I haven't decided if I like it enough to finish it yet."

"OK. Well, you let me know," I say, giving her one last smile before I pull her door closed and head into my bedroom for that much-needed shower.

By the time I'm finished, Mom is plating up our meal and Leah is setting knives and forks on the table.

"This looks wonderful, Mom," I say of the stuffed pork chops with green beans and mashed potato she's made for our dinner. And it goes down a treat after we say grace and make small talk, doing our best to draw Leah into the conversation but failing miserably. We're lucky to get grunts or single-word answers out of her. But in the end, she gets up and clears all the plates from the table and cleans the kitchen before thanking Mom for the food and disappearing back into her room again.

Still in shock over my daughter's actions, Mom and I pour a glass of wine and move to the living room.

"Do we call that progress?" I ask as we relax into our separate seats.

"Progress, groveling, bribery...it's all the same really," she says, a cheeky glint in her eye as she sips from her glass. "Have you had any more thoughts about what you're gonna do once the two weeks are up?"

Shaking my head, I take a drink, then cradle the glass in my lap. "I'm starting to think you're more of a superwoman than I first thought. That's all I know right now."

Mom laughs and holds out her arm to clink her glass with mine. "I'll drink to that, but also, apart from the whole 'Mom I'm pregnant' bomb you dropped on me at fifteen, you weren't *that* bad." I shoot her a pointed look. "I did say *that* bad. You were rebellious, but not to the point of putting your safety at risk. And back then, we didn't even have all the technology you have now. It makes it harder to know what they're *really* doing."

"I know. It's just... What do I do, Mom? As much as I'd love to lock her up in her room until she's twenty-five and has her head on straight, I know I can't do that."

"Well, yes. That kind of thing *is* frowned upon these days."

"And I know she's growing up and part of that is making decisions for herself and making mistakes, but it's just..."

"The difference this time, Eleanor, is that she put herself in harm's way, and as far as I can recall, she still hasn't apologized for it. Which means she's still at the angry stage, not the remorseful one. And that's something that just cannot fly. Because our girl up there"—she looks toward the staircase before turning her eyes back to meet mine–"is a sweetheart. We just have to give her time to find that in herself again." I smile because she's right. We've been holding out hope that Leah would snap out of whatever *phase* this is because occasionally we'll get glimpses of the kind, considerate, reliable, and loyal girl we've raised together. "It may not seem like it right now, but behind that closed door is still the little girl with the bouncy brown pigtails who would run out into the garden and pick us a daisy each for our hair, and who'd crawl into your bed in the middle of a thunderstorm. She's the girl who'd beg to bake cookies with me on Sunday mornings and who spent hours drawing and coloring a homemade 'Leah McIntyre special' Mother's Day card for you every year."

"I'm starting to think about moving her away from Timber Falls. Maybe a fresh start and new surroundings will help Leah find herself again? But the more I dwell on that, the more I wonder if maybe that's overkill."

"Is it though?" Mom replies, making my whole body jerk as I study her face, wondering if I misheard her.

"Really? You think that's what I should do?"

"Yeah. It would depend on where you wanted to go, of course. But moving out of the district so she's attending a different school could be the fresh start she needs. I don't think that's a bad idea at all."

"You don't think it's crazy? Bonkers? Maybe a little *extreme*?" I can feel my eyes popping out of my head the more I realize that Mom isn't just placating me. She's being one hundred percent real. "Mom, c'mon. Think about it. We'd be uprooting her from everything she's ever known. The only *house* she's ever lived in."

"Yep. And we'd be putting distance between her and her friends, and that troublemaker boyfriend of hers who comes up with hair-brained ideas like hitching a train to *Anchorage* with your sixteen-year-old daughter. Sorry, Nora, but even *you* in your wildest days wouldn't have traveled *that* far away from home without me knowing about it. You were wild, you weren't god damn out of your mind." As she speaks, it hits me that I've never seen Mom this riled up about something before. She was disappointed in me plenty of times while growing up, sure. But right now, she seems *pissed* and willing to do anything to help set Leah straight.

"What if she hates me for it?" I whisper, verbalizing one of my biggest fears.

Mom's matching green eyes soften as she reaches over and gives my shoulder a gentle squeeze. "Put it this way. If I had the option and means to do so, I would've done the exact same thing you're contemplating now when you were Leah's age. And you've got yourself to think about now too, Nora. I don't want whatever this thing with Leah is to make you pull back and not keep seeing where things with Randy could go. You're thirty-one, you're beautiful, you're accomplished and successful in your career, and you've liked this man for a long time. You've got a good life already, and if you moved to a place like…Kinleyville, for example, just imagine what it could be like with a good man by your side too? You owe it to yourself to find a way to help your daughter *and* get what you want at the same time."

I think of that for a moment, loving the belief Mom has in me. "Do you think me seeing Randy is what made her act out so big this time?"

"No. You don't get to do that, Eleanor. You don't take any of the blame for your daughter's choices on your shoulders. This is on her, because we both know she was raised better than how she's acting right now. Our job is to guide and teach her, and you not following your feelings for a man who's clearly as into you as you're into him, well what would that teach Leah? It would teach her that throwing tantrums gets her something."

I open my mouth to speak, but sensing she's on a roll, I close it again.

"Nope," Mom continues. "Don't even try to justify what I know you're probably thinking. You putting your life on hold and dedicating everything to this family and your daughter *has* taught her one thing–that she is loved. And I bet that even if you asked her straight, she'd never want you to sacrifice your happiness just because she's going through a rough patch.

She's sixteen, not six. You've done the hard time, and take it from someone who's been there and lived to tell the tale all these years afterward. Children are best taught by action, by seeing the adults in their lives actually *live* their lives. It's leading by example and you've done a damn fine job of it so far. Don't start doubting yourself just because you've reached a bump in the road."

"I guess *your* bump in the road was a literal bump with me," I say, smirking as I mime a rounded belly for her.

Mom arches a brow and looks as unimpressed as a person can pretend to be while smiling. "Indeed. And as much as I love that girl to bits and wouldn't change anything that happened for the world, maybe a change of scenery, school, and friends–boyfriends, especially–might just help us avoid another literal bump in the future."

"Oh god! Don't even put that thought into the universe," I gasp, taking a big gulp of my wine. I'm thirty-one and *far* too young to be a grandmother.

Mom points to me. "That reaction right there, that thought, the fact that it's even within the realm of possibility, is exactly why I think we *should* move. Maybe we can think of it as a new adventure for the McIntyre girls. We've handled everything life's thrown at us so far. There's no reason we can't best this little challenge."

"But what about my work, my business, my clients?"

"Kinleyville isn't that far. You can commute when need be and work from home the rest of the time. There are video calls, emails. Hell, I've even heard some people still pick up the phone to talk on occasion these days." I scoff and roll my eyes. *She's not wrong.*

"What I'm saying, my sweet girl, is everything and anything is possible. And what's the worst that could happen—it doesn't work out and we move back here? But at the best? Well, the sky's the limit. And if it helps Leah, and helps *you* learn to live as a *woman* as well as a mom, then I can't see why the hell not. Hell, maybe I need a change of scenery too. Been living in this town for far too long now. I'd love to try out some new pastures."

With her words swirling around in my head, I lean back against the couch and sip at the last of my wine. "I guess I have some thinking to do," I say, nodding as I meet Mom's eyes.

"And I trust that no matter which way you go, you'll do it knowing what's best."

## 14

## RANDY

Between my duties at the ranch and knowing Nora and Leah would need a few days as a family, I've managed to keep myself busy while giving the woman who's never left my mind for a minute some space. Sure, I checked in on her to make sure she was OK, but when I was sitting at my desk late last night crunching numbers and working out the ranch's feed requirements for the coming month, I realized 'checking in' just wasn't cutting it. It wasn't just that I *wanted* to see Nora again. It was this overwhelming, undeniable feeling that I *needed* to. And soon...

After spending the night mulling over whether I should just wait it out or take action, I decided that waiting is the reason it took so long for something to happen between us in the first place. And now that we are dating each other, navigating the change in our relationship from purely professional to a much more enjoyable personal one, I don't want to waste any more time. Not with Nora, not with how important she's coming to be to me.

So, as soon as I was finished with my chores, I called her office and made sure I scheduled some time to see her just before lunch. Her assistant, Diana, promised to keep it a surprise and assured me she'd make herself scarce.

I'm aching to see Nora. At the very least, I need to see her with my own eyes and make sure she's OK. But I also need to touch her, comfort her, and show her that I'm not going anywhere.

"Ah, here's our fearless leader," my brother, Sawyer, says as though he's commentating a nature documentary when I step out of the house, dressed and ready to head to Timber Falls. "Randy is the oldest male of the Barnes clan, and he's sporting a strange curve to his lips, rarely seen around these parts. Some would call it a smile. Others would call it gas." He leans in and elbows our cousin, Jasper, who nudges Beau while they all erupt into laughter, stuffing their faces with sandwiches from *my* kitchen on the front porch of *my* house. Can't say I'm surprised.

"Havin' a nice time there, you three?" I ask, crossing my arms and planting my feet in the gravel in front of them, deciding I may as well let them get this out of their systems. Seems impossible to go anywhere or do anything on this ranch without someone having their say.

"He's dressed in his best green plaid shirt too," Jasper says, joining in.

Sawyer nods slowly. "Those are his goin' out boots and Levis, too. Got somethin' or someone on your mind, brother?"

Beau looks at me and rolls his eyes. "Leave 'im be," he says to the other two. "Randy deserves some privacy just as much as the rest of us. The Call's no joke when you're goin' through it."

"Sure is sweet when you get to the other side though," Jesse says, emerging from the kitchen door with a sandwich in hand, earning grunts of agreement from the three other men who have, in fact, 'gone through it.'

"Don't recall mentionin' to a single one of you that this thing is the Call," I say, pulling my hat from my head and running a hand through my hair. "I'm just headin' into town, is all. I'll be back when I'm back."

"Back from where?" our sister, Ellie-Mae, pops her head out the door, obviously on her tiptoes so she can see over Jesse's shoulder.

"Give him some privacy!" Beau repeats, making me smirk.

"He can have privacy," Sawyer puts in before a smirk takes over his mouth. "When he finally admits this thing with his accountant *is* the Call. He can have *all* the privacy he needs then. Hell, I'll even pick up your chores, Randy. Far be it for me to stand between a man and his ability to take care of his woman." All eyes turn my way, watching me expectantly for a comeback.

"I'm taking the *smartest* brother's advice on this one." My eyes move to Beau's before returning to the rest of them. "A man *does* deserve privacy, so I'm gonna take it. But I will tell y'all this–I'm interested in Nora, and we're datin' and seein' where things might lead. *But* we're takin' it slow since she has an impressionable and somewhat troubled daughter, which is where her focus needs to be right now. That's something I'm more than OK with because everything I know of Nora so far is telling me the wait will be more than worth it."

The baying for blood look in the men's eyes vanishes in front of my eyes. Respect, surprise, and understanding taking its place.

Sawyer gets to his feet and moves my way, clapping my shoulder. "I'll still do your jobs, Rand. You go see your girl. We've got things handled here. Nothin' more important than family. We all know that."

"I'm on my phone if ya need me," I say as get in my truck and head in the direction of Timber Falls. For the first time in a few days, the weird tightness in my chest starts to ease the closer I get to Nora.

∼

"Just the man I was hoping to see," Nora says with a huge smile on her face when I stroll into her office with a brown bag with takeout sushi in my hand. Of all things I thought I'd never like to eat, raw fish and rice wrapped in seaweed was definitely at the top of that list, but here I am.

"You knew I was comin'?" I ask, wondering if Diana let the cat out of the sushi bag as I drop the food onto her desk.

"No." She stands and meets me halfway. "I've just been thinking about you non-stop. I'm always hoping I'll look up and you'll be right there." Loving the words coming out of her mouth, I wrap my arms around her, looping her raven hair around my fist and tilting her mouth up just in time for me to slam my lips down on hers, growling when her body melts against mine as her hands grip my shoulders, holding on for dear life.

Needing air far too soon for my liking, I tear my mouth away and stare into those stunning sage eyes of hers. "Hey, darlin'."

She grins up at me, her pink lips puffy and swollen from my attention. *And by god, is that a good look on her.* "Damn, Randy. You can come in here and kiss me like that any time."

Chuckling, I give her one last peck to tide me over and shift back. "That's an open invitation I'll never turn down."

"Good." She shuffles back to lean her perfectly round butt against the top of her desk as I grab the food and pull it out of the bag, holding out what Diana assured me was Nora's favorite 'lunch on the go–avocado and crab sushi. Nora's eyes light up. "How did you know?"

Handing it over, I wink and tap my nose. "A gentleman must never reveal *all* his secrets."

She narrows her eyes at me, then giggles. "Remind me to give Diana a raise for not only surprising me with my favorite appointment of the day, but also being a secret source to you for all things me."

"And she very kindly left the office so we'd have a little quiet time, just the two of us."

Nora's beautiful, breathtaking smile comes back out to play. "Oh, she's definitely getting a raise then."

Unable to resist, I reach out and gently grip her chin before stealing another brush of a kiss and taking my lunch with me as I sit in the chair opposite her, both of us eating in comfortable silence for a spell.

"So how're things with Leah after her little adventure?" I ask, wiping my mouth with a napkin and setting my empty container aside. Turns out, sushi doesn't taste half bad.

"It's only been a few days, so she's still rather quiet. But she's also being the dutiful daughter by doing all her chores and then some. So that's a plus. I'm just worried that I'll relax for a moment and she'll sneak out with that boy when I'm not looking."

"So typical teenage behavior, then? Even when they're *not* grounded?"

"Pretty much!" she replies with a laugh. "But surely they're not *all* this hard."

"My experience with teenagers is long past now that my brothers and cousins are all grown, but yeah, they were all hard."

"God." She places a hand against her cheek as she groans. "Why can't this part of life be as easy as when they're little and all their tantrums center around candy and going to bed? At least it settles down and they turn out OK in the end, right?"

"Let's see. Out of eight Barnes brothers and cousins, plus our adopted sister Ellie-Mae, there's only one who still likes to cause trouble."

"Remy?"

"Yeah," I say, flashing her a smile as she nods knowingly, since I had to ask her to release some funds so I could post bail for him a while back. "Seems that one is a magnet for poor decisions. But the rest seemed to find their feet after a little hard work and guidance, so I think we're doing OK."

"For what it's worth, I think you've done an amazing job taking on the role of head of the family. Can't have been easy when you were grieving yourself."

"We all do what we have to do," I say. "I make it a point to always be available for the people I care about."

A small smile curves her mouth as she places her chopsticks on the side of her almost-empty sushi container. "Which is why I wanted to thank you again for coming to mine and Leah's rescue the other day. I really appreciated it. I hope you know that."

"I do," I say, meeting her warm eyes and feeling heat and affection building in mine. "And it was no trouble. I want to be here for you when you need me. Both of you."

"Bet you didn't bargain for a single mom with a teenager daughter when you asked me out–"

"Stop right there, Nora," I say before she can go any further in the wrong direction. "There ain't nothin' about you that has, will, or could ever put me off the idea of makin' you mine." I stand, my eyes locked with her widening ones as I close the distance between us, grateful she's wearing a skirt with splits on the side–and not just for the glimpse of her silky pale skin it gives–but also cause it allows her to accommodate me as I stand between her legs and brace my hands on the desk beside her. "And part of being with you, dating you, seeing where this feelin' between us takes us *is* Leah. And your mom. And *my* family. All of them. We're all part of the package." Her breath catches while I speak, but then I watch mesmerized as her glassy eyes start to crinkle at the sides and a smile curves her lips before she cups my bearded jaw and kisses me, soft and slow, her tongue seeking mine and caressing it with gentle probing licks that has my body firing up quicker than dry hay in the hot summer sun.

When we pull away breathless, Nora's arms reluctantly let me go. "I like you a lot, Randy Barnes."

"Mmm. I like you more than a lot, Nora. Which is why I really wanna do something more to help you with your...current situation," I start, licking my lips as I broach a topic that could be seen as overstepping the mark,

"My current situation?" she repeats. "Do you mean Leah?"

"I do," I start, holding a hand up like I'm approaching a restless mare. "Now, I preface this by sayin' that this offer comes from a place carin' and compassion because I've helped set unruly teens straight in the past, but if this isn't somethin' you wanna explore, then there's no pressure. OK? The choice is one hundred percent yours." Her brows pinch together before she nods her agreement.

"I'm listening."

"What if you move to Kinleyville and let Leah work for me as a ranch hand?" Nora's eyes go wide and her mouth opens, but I hold my hand up to silence her this time so I can finish before she airs any objections. "In my experience, a little hard work and responsibility can do wonders for someone in need of a little direction. And giving Leah a fresh start away from current influences could be just the thing she needs. My brother, Beau, and his wife Molly have a house that's sitting empty since their last tenants relocated for work. It's a four-bedroom cottage sitting on a small parcel of land not far from the town center, and I think it'd be perfect for y'all if you're interested. It's on the school bus route and also close enough for your Mom to walk into town to socialize. They'd be more than happy to let you use the place."

"Oh, Randy," she gasps. "I couldn't ask that of Beau and Molly. That's far too generous."

There's my girl, strong and independent. I cup her shoulders in my hands and give a gentle squeeze. "Then you can pay rent just like any other tenant. I know this might mean a fair bit of commuting to and from the office, but it's a good town, not too much trouble, and the high school is well respected in these parts. Molly's sister, Sage, is a senior there, and her youngest brother, Cody, will be going there when he's of age as well. Sage has her head screwed on straight, so she could help Leah acclimatize if need be. And I know it's a big change, but I thought maybe it could be an option worth thinkin' about."

"Interestingly enough, Mom and I talked about something like this last night–moving to a new town, I mean. She thinks getting Leah out of Timber Falls to start fresh could be the right thing to do."

"And you, darlin'. What do *you* think?"

A dry snort escapes her. "I think my daughter could end up hating me before she starts liking me again, if I'm being honest. But after her last stunt in Anchorage, I can't help but think something has got to give. And I do like the idea of her working as a ranch hand. I think that could really teach her a lot about the world."

"What about you personally? Your business? Your clients?"

"Well, there are lots of ways around that hurdle. Plus, one of my *favorite* clients just happens to live right near Kinleyville, and I'll tell you a little secret," she says, leaning in, "I happen to have a mighty big crush on the guy so maybe... just maybe... if we were all living closer to each other, we might be able to give this dating thing a real shot."

A satisfied growl rumbles deep in my chest. "I have it on pretty good authority that he'd like that."

"I think I'd like that too," she whispers, sliding her arms up over my shoulders. "I'd like that a hell of a lot." She kisses me again, wilder than the last, getting me hot and heavy and wanting all over again. *God, this woman is gonna make me burn right up in a minute.*

"I think I'll take that as a 'you'll at least consider it' then?" I state, my lips brushing against hers as I speak.

"We'll be having a McIntyre family meeting as soon as I get home tonight, but your offer is definitely high on the list of options for us all to consider. Thank you," she says, her eyes bright. "How did I get so lucky to catch the attention of a wonderful man like you, Randy Barnes?"

"I dunno. But I'm startin' to think that maybe the Mountain had something to do with it."

"The M?" She chuckles, her brow knitting in slight confusion as I grin down at her.

"I'll explain it all later, darlin'," I say, checking my watch before pulling her in a little closer. "Your lunch break is almost over, so no more talkin'. We're gonna spend the rest of the hour making out instead."

"Fine by me," she rushes out before I take her mouth in mine and lose myself completely in the taste and feel of her. My mind, my body, and my soul have never felt more alive in my forty-eight-year-long life.

## 15

## NORA

Driving along the road on our way toward the ranch for Leah's first day of work with Randy, I'm cautiously optimistic that maybe–just maybe–this might be the start of a new passion for Leah.

Although it might result in a new pin being stuck into her figurative mom voodoo doll too if the scowl on her face from the passenger seat is anything to go by.

It's been a few days since Mom, Leah, and I made the big shift from Timber Falls to Kinleyville. The morning of moving day, Randy turned up behind the wheel of a big furniture truck, closely followed by two vehicles full of his burly brothers and cousins, announcing that all we had to do was direct the Barnes's men where to go and what to move where. I could've jumped into the man's arms and kissed him right there in front of everyone, and the look he shot me in return assured me that the feeling was absolutely mutual.

From there, we watched as our whole life in Timber Falls and everything we'd gathered over the years was packed up and then driven toward a fresh start in a new town.

And an hour later, when we pulled into the driveway of Molly and Beau's rental–our new home–it still felt surreal as we unloaded everything and set about *creating* our new life. Elle-Mae, bless her heart, even arrived on our doorstep that same night with enough meals and food to keep us going for a few days, because in her words, "Randy said we have to let y'all settle in before we start initiatin' you girls into the Kinleyville way of life, but since nobody wants to be unpackin' *and* havin' to worry about cookin', this was the most he'd let me do."

That made the guys chuckle, Mum giggle, Leah's lips twitch, and Randy groan and look to the ceiling, an adorable pink coloring his skin beneath his bearded cheeks.

Then they all left us to it, Randy asking me to walk him out before he did what might just be the most swoon-worthy, sexy, butterflies-in-my-tummy thing he's ever done. He gave me a hug and a kiss on the cheek, and then explained that he would give me and Leah time to get settled in the new house, school, and work arrangements, but that he'd be checking in with me daily. He asked me to promise to do the same. I felt so well cared for, that if we didn't have what I knew was an avid audience of his family *and* undoubtedly mine, I would've jumped into his arms right there in my new driveway and done everything I've been dreaming about doing with him since he hinted at a grown-up sleepover all those weeks ago.

But alas, I didn't. And as much as I could tell by the look in his eyes that he was wanting that same thing, we both knew it'd have to keep waiting and simmering in the forefronts of our minds until my life became something a little more manageable than it is right now. While Mom was right about the fact that I deserve to have a life too, Leah does need my focus right now. And knowing that the man I want to explore having that life with is one hundred percent willing to wait and support me through my troubles tells me that Randy Barnes is the one and only man I'd ever consider building a life with. He's a once-in-a-lifetime human, that man. And I find myself falling harder and harder for him every day, maybe not even still falling... maybe I'm already gone for him.

One thing I have been mindful of during this whole life upheaval has been Leah. The night I came home from the office and broke the news of my decision to move with her and Mom, tears filled her eyes as she begged and pleaded with me not to take her away from her friends. *"Mom, I'll be good. I promise. Please."*

It didn't matter how much Mom and I both assured her that it was the best thing, for not just her but all three of us, she kept apologizing and trying to get me to change my mind.

"I think you'll really enjoy the ranch, sweetheart," I say, looking out for the turn that'll lead me down the valley toward the ranch's entry gate.

Leah snorts. "Unlikely, Nora." Yeah, I'm back to being Nora to her, too. That whole 'Mom' thing was a one-night-only appearance, apparently.

I reach over and squeeze her knee. "You never know. Have you ever *been* a ranch hand before?"

"Well *duh*, of course I haven't. But I've watched cowboy shows to know I'll hate it. The ranch hands get treated like shit and they're made to do *all* the work nobody else wants to."

"Language, Leah," I warn in a low whisper.

"Whatever. You know as well as I do that ranch hands are like the lowest of the low. I'm not sure in what universe you're living in to think I'd ever *enjoy* it. God, knowing my luck, your *boyfriend* will probably have me shoveling shi–*manure*–every damn minute of the day."

As hard as I try, I can't stop the giggle escaping my pursed lips, earning an exasperated teenage sigh from the fruit of my loins.

And not for the first time since I told my daughter about working at the ranch, I realize that there's nothing I can say that will have any effect on Leah's mood or attitude toward her new weekend 'job'. But regardless, I still think it'll do her the world of good.

I've spent a lot of time thinking about what Mom could have done to stop me rebelling and getting into trouble when I was younger, what it would've taken to get my head screwed on straight and to focus on the future rather than the 'right now,' and every time, I reach the same conclusion. Had Mom uprooted my life, moved towns, and found me a job that would take up my spare time *and* wear me out so that I was too tired to even contemplate sneaking out or hanging with friends late into the night, the direction my life took from age fifteen onward would have been a lot different.

I wouldn't change having Leah in my life for the world. I love her more than anything. First and foremost, I'm a mother and Leah is my reason for everything. But I'm also a Mama Bear that will do anything and everything required to make life better for my daughter *and* my mom–because lord knows I put her through enough over the years and she's never once not had my back. That means sacrifices and hard decisions, and doing them whether Leah agrees it's right or not. That's what anyone does for the people they love, and sometimes you have to be the bad guy to do it.

My only hope is that eventually, Leah might realize that all we're trying to do is help her find the right path and realize that life is her oyster. All she needs to do is open her eyes, her heart, and her mind.

And if she's not ready to do that, then maybe some hard manual labor might just help her get there.

"How long am I doing this thing for, anyway?"

Spotting the arch at the start of the ranch's driveway, I turn our car down the long, sweeping dirt road toward the buildings. "Today? I think until about seven."

"That late?"

"I seem to remember you like hanging out late."

"Mom!" she growls–yes, *growls*. "Be *serious*! I'll miss dinner."

Now it's my turn to sigh. "You work for the ranch now, sweetheart. You'll be here whenever

Randy needs you to be and stay until he says you're done. They'll feed you here the same as everyone else, and when you're through with all your chores, I'll pick you up and take you home."

"But–"

"Leah, just please give it a chance. If not for me, then do it for yourself. You've always liked animals, and this just happens to be a ranch that has a lot of them."

"A lot of their poop all over the place to scoop up too, I bet," she grumbles.

I chuckle. "Probably. But ranch hands do a lot more than just shovel poop. If you give this a chance, who knows what you might learn? You might even like farming life."

Snorting, she shakes her head. "Doubt *that* will ever happen. I'm just here to do whatever you and your boyfriend are making me do, then go home and do it all over again until you say I don't have to anymore." I pull the car to a stop outside a big white wooden ranch house, smiling at the sight of the hat-wearing, plaid shirt-donned, denim-clad cowboy that miraculously–or stupidly–wants to take on my attitude-filled offspring.

"Look at you drooling over him. He looks like a muscly scarecrow in that shirt and hat. *Gross*."

Her nose scrunches up and her mouth twists in apparent disgust at her mother having a pulse. "Should I leave you two alone? Maybe you can drive your car behind the barn and make out back *there* this time."

As much as I want to laugh, I somehow manage to keep a straight face as I turn my attention from the sexy cowboy walking our way to Leah. "That's enough of that, sweetheart."

"Whatever. Just don't take me being here as a win in the parenting stakes, OK?"

This time I let my lips curl up into a lop-sided smile. "Then why *are* you here, Leah Melody McIntyre? Could it be 'cause you're curious?"

Her green eyes widen before narrowing, a mumbled, "ugh!" escaping her lips.

She reaches for her door handle, and I reach out to touch her arm, succeeding in getting her attention. "Leah, whatever happens, you *will* be respectful and use your manners while you're here. You will listen to and do whatever Randy orders you to, and you'll do it with a smile. Do you understand?"

Her eyes flash with what I hope is understanding before she mutters, "Whatever," and quickly hops out of the car, making her way toward the porch where Randy still stands, his gaze locked on mine.

I look over at him, both loving and regretting the longing look he's sending me. I love it because I feel just the same as he does, and I regret it because right now there's nothing we can do to act on our feelings–even *if* her idea of making out behind the barn was a distinct possibility.

"I miss you," I mouth to him, not missing the spark of desire in his eyes as he reads my lips. Because I do, even though he's right in front of me and we live closer than before, he's giving me the space I need to take care of my daughter, and also taking her on here at the ranch.

Hell, *Leah* is getting to spend more alone time with my man than I am!

I see him say something to Leah as she stops in front of him before he reaches into his pocket, pulls out his cell, and types something into his phone. A second later, my phone vibrates in the center console. And when I open my messages, there's no stopping the smile that takes over my face.

**Randy: I miss you too.**

**Nora: Please accept my apologies in advance for my daughter's attitude.**

**Randy: She's not my first feisty mare, and I'm sure she won't be my last.**

That makes me giggle and I watch the man I whole-lot-more-than-like, grin at me through the windscreen.

**Nora: Take care of my girl for me, Randy.**

**Randy: Like she was my own, darlin'. Trust me.**

# 16

## RANDY

"What are you gruntin' and growlin' about there, Randy?" Ellie-Mae asks as I stomp about the kitchen, trying to find the lid for my thermos so I can take a much-needed mug of cowboy coffee out into the yard with me while I wrangle a surly teen for the fourth weekend in a row.

"I need a lid for this." I lift my arm above the cupboard I'm searching in so she can see the thermos in my hand.

"Oh, that's in the cutlery drawer." She plucks the stainless-steel mug from my hand and glides across the kitchen to the stove, filling my cup then pulling the lid from the drawer and capping it for me. "There ya go. Coffee for the man on a mission." As I reach out to take it, she quickly thrusts a cheese and herb muffin my way as well. "A little food to balance out all that caffeine, too."

"Thank you," I grunt, taking both items and biting into the muffin, the heavy sweetness of the herby cheese coating my tongue and making me a little calmer. Cheese-anything seems to be magic like that. "This is good."

"Oh, I know," she says, shooting me a smile over her shoulder as she measures out rolled oats and drops them into a pot. "You wanna get somethin' off your chest? Or you just wanna stand there watchin' me work?" My sister has never been one to ignore an elephant in a room, no matter how big or small. And this past month living so close to Nora but having very little contact with her while she focuses on getting Leah settled into school and life in a new town. The giant elephant in the room is my bad mood. I miss her. So much that I ache for every moment I get to spend near her. Phone calls and brief meetings just aren't enough anymore.

I glance over my shoulder and out the open door, knowing Leah is currently waiting for me in the barn. It's not that I dislike the girl—far from it. If she could just get out of her own way for a few seconds, I think she'd have a good head on her shoulders and the ability to succeed at anything she puts her mind to. But so far, getting her to do much of anything has been as fun as pushing against a mule that doesn't want to budge. She speaks in monosyllables and purposely does a terrible job no matter how many times I show her how to get it done right the first time. It's like she thinks that the worse she does, the faster I'll give up and just send her back home to her mother. But the jokes on her because I'm more stubborn than any mule and definitely more steadfast than any surly teenager. She's going to have a long fight on her hands if she thinks she's going to win against me. I care about her mother more than I care for myself, so I'm in this for the long haul.

"No, not really," I say, biting into the muffin again. "Just mentally preparin' myself for the workday."

"Girl's still givin' you trouble, hey?" Ellie says, stirring in some milk before firing up the burner. She doesn't look at me when she speaks, but I can tell by the set of her shoulders that she knows enough to be worried. Ellie-Mae has a kind heart and likes to be a mother-type figure to everyone she meets. Having conversed with Nora and learning the kind of girl Leah was before—sweet and quiet and so shy you couldn't get a word out of her for love nor money—it tugs at her heartstrings to see the child so obviously confused and in pain. Leah's so caught up in this new tough-as-nails persona she's adopted that it's like she'd rather be angry than accept a single iota of help from those around her. And while I think some of it is just teenage hormones and moods, I also can't forget how distraught her mother was when she ran off to Anchorage and got picked up by the police. I don't ever want to see Nora going through that heartache again. So, no matter how hard Leah pushes, I'm gonna just keep on standing firm. I know deep in my heart that all of us here on the Eagle Mountain Ranch can make this right. Not just for the sake of Leah, but for my relationship with Nora, too. We all deserve a chance here. *The Mountain would never steer us wrong.*

"Yeah. But she'll come around," I grumble, taking a gulp of the coffee before setting my muffin down on the table and heading toward the mudroom door that leads outside. "It's like breakin' in a new horse. You gotta keep at 'em and show 'em who's boss."

"Hmm. It's been a solid month now, though, and you're not really makin' much headway. You ever think it might be fun to give up the tough-guy act and let yourself be vulnerable around her? Talk about your past. Maybe she'll respond to that?"

"That doesn't sound even slightly fun," I grumble again, grabbing my hat off a hook and thrusting it on my head before heading out into the bright morning sun. I can see Leah's shadowy outline through the open barn doors, but I can also see she's in there with someone else. That causes me to frown because I don't remember scheduling any of the boys in the barn today. I marked that on the schedule for just Leah and me.

"You go ridin' a lot?" I hear Leah ask, her voice lighter and more friendly than I've ever heard it.

"Every single day, sugar," the other, very familiar voice of Beau's brother-in-law, Colton, replies. *Sugar?* I quicken my pace as I realize I failed to consider the possibility of the teenage Colton crossing paths with the impressionable and easily distracted Leah. *Shoot.*

I know Colton to be a good man and all, but Leah doesn't need anyone sweet-talking to her about anything. She came here to get her head on straight, not for us to present her with another reason to have it up in the clouds, pining for a boy who's far too old for a sixteen-year-old. *Well, only four years older, but that's like ten in teenage years, right?*

"I wish I could go riding. I love horses. But so far, Randy's only letting me clean up their dung."

Colton chuckles. "Oh yeah. I remember doin' that my first days here. I got myself in trouble takin' my sister's car when I shouldn't have. My sister, Molly, was kinda seein' Randy's brother —Beau—at the time. So he called in a favor, got the car fixed, and me and my siblings worked on the ranch to pay for the repairs."

"How long ago was that?"

"A good year and a half now," Colton replies, and I decide to hang back, knowing this conversation could be just the thing she needs to hear.

"Oh, my god. Must have been some car!"

"Nah." Colton shakes his head. "I just came to love it so much here that I decided to stay."

"You *wanted* to stay?" Leah balks. "I can't imagine choosing this place. It's so...dirty."

"Ah, but there're horses to ride, Gators to drive, cows to raise, great people, and best of all—Ellie-Mae's huckleberry pies paired with copious amounts of her cowboy coffee. I'd go as far as callin' this place a slice of Paradise. Especially since there's a water—"

"You two gettin' along OK?" I ask, letting myself be known before Colton lets the cat out of the bag by telling Leah about the secret little spot to the edge of our property dubbed Paradise Springs. Those of us who believe in the Mountain Spirit and all of Her divinity count that place as sacred. The only time we take someone outside the family there is when we feel sure they've been brought to us by the Call. Leah isn't old enough to visit a place like that with my nineteen-year-old brother-in-law. Not yet. Maybe never...

"She was just askin' me about life on the ranch," Colton says, swiping a hand across the light smattering of golden stubble on his jaw.

I pin him with a stare that speaks volumes about what I think about him chatting up my young charge. "Don't you have chores that need attendin' to?"

"Ah, yeah." He smiles. "Was just gettin' a new lead." He gestures to his mare and checks the new lead is clipped onto the bridle, nice and tight. "Mine snapped."

"Looks like that's fixed now."

"Guess I should be pushin' on, then." Colton looks at Leah and pops a dimple. "Maybe I can take you ridin' sometime."

"She's sixteen." I snap out a warning before Leah can even respond. "Don't even think about takin' her anywhere."

Colton nods his understanding and climbs up onto his horse, saying a fast goodbye as he heads out of the barn.

What was supposed to be a blush on Leah's face turns into embarrassment and possibly fury as her eyes land on mine. "What'd you have to go and do that for?" she demands. "He was the first cool person I've met since stepping foot in this podunk town."

"You're sixteen, and he's too old for you. And on top of that, it's not a podunk town—it's the best place this side of heaven."

"Because of the Mountain Spirit?" She puts her hands on her hips and juts out her chin. "I've heard you all talkin' like it's some kinda magic genie granting you wishes. You're all worried about me at sixteen, but aren't you a little old to be believin' in magic and unicorns, Ran-dy?" she says, accentuating my name.

I let out a sigh. "I don't expect you to understand our beliefs, Leah. But I'd like it if you could at least respect them."

"I don't even know what they are."

"We believe that the Mountain protects and takes care of us."

She scoffs. "Does my mom know you're this crazy?"

"Somewhat," I say, a hand lifting to the back of my neck and rubbing as I make a mental note to sit down with Nora and fully explain our family's lore before she hears a twisted-up version from her daughter.

Leah folds her arms now and laughs. "She has no idea, does she? She thinks you're some kind-hearted, god-fearing rancher, and it turns out you worship a *mountain*." Her eyes go wide. "Oh, my god! Is this Mountain Spirit like the one in those romance books?" The look on my face answers for me, and she laughs again. "Oh wow. So does this mean you believe my mom was called to you by the Mountain?"

"Somethin' like that," I admit, shuffling on my feet. "And I don't appreciate you laughin' at it like it's somethin' to be ashamed of or mocked. It's how Ellie-Mae and Miller were bought together, and three of my other brothers and their wives, along with my cousin Jasper and his new wife, Sarah."

She continues like I didn't say a word. "It's pretty ridiculous, Randy. And Nora stopped believing in fairy tales when I turned up and ruined all her plans."

"Is that how you see yourself?" I ask, my eyes narrowing slightly as she reveals a little something about her inner workings.

"Well, she freaked the fuck out over me gettin' a boyfriend. It's her worst nightmare to have her own daughter become a teen mom. So you know what that means, right? It means she regrets having me."

"That's not true at all, Leah."

"Really? Then why are we here, Randy? Why did Nora move me away from everything I've ever known to force me to work myself exhausted so I don't even have time to think about boys?"

"Because despite lovin' you to the ends of the earth, Leah, your mother wants to give you a life that's even better than hers."

Bouncing a shoulder, she turns away and picks up a broom and muck bucket. "Funny. Because I always thought we had a pretty awesome life. Guess I was wrong."

And as I watch her move around in the horse stall cleaning it out, I feel like I'm starting to understand exactly what went wrong. Pulling out my phone, I shoot Nora a quick message.

**Me: I need to see you**

**Nora: I need to see you too.**

I smile at her fast reply.

**Me: Tonight? After Leah has gone to bed?**

**Nora: Around 11? Is that too late?**

**Me: Never. See you then.**

**Nora: Can't wait.**

As I slide my cell back into my pocket, I let out a sigh filled with tense longing. Leah was right that Nora might think I'm crazy in my beliefs. I need to explain this whole Mountain Call thing to her, and in the same breath, I need to tell her that I think her daughter's attitude is coming from her fear that maybe her mom didn't really want her. This isn't going to be an easy conversation, but if we get through it unscathed, then my mind will be made up and I'll know without a doubt that Nora is my one and I'll do whatever it takes to keep her.

But if I'm honest, I'm already ninety-nine point nine percent there, anyway.

## 17

## NORA

Randy: Psst. I have a great idea. Wanna sneak out with me? I'm in your driveway *wink emoji*

I frown at my phone as I sit cross-legged and fully dressed on my bed, everyone else in the house safe and sound in bed. *I thought the plan was to sneak out?*

Nora: Randy... did you just send me an emoji like a teenager? *laugh emoji*

Randy: Spend enough time with Colton and Sage and you too would be learning emoji speak.

Nora: I have Leah, I'm well adept at emojis.

Randy: Well how about you get that sweet ass of yours out here and into my truck? There's something I wanna show you.

**Nora: That's what all the boys say *devil emoji* On my way.**

Reminiscent of my teenage years when I'd wait till Mom was sound asleep, I quietly make my way out of my bedroom toward the front door, letting the dim light from inside the cab of Randy's idling truck guide me once I'm outside.

When I close the door behind me, Randy's earthy scent, so quintessentially him, reaches my nose. And I suddenly feel calm and centered. It's surreal but when we both lean in and touch our lips together, my mind clears, all of my worries disappearing as my heart skips a beat and my stomach flips, my entire body warming from the inside out as my soul recognizes I'm exactly where I'm meant to be and with exactly who I'm meant to be with. As the kiss turns from soft and gentle to deep and passionate, I can barely stop myself from begging him for more.

Kissing Randy Barnes is something I am still not used to. The way he holds me in place and nearly consumes me with his mouth is a heady feeling.

"Darlin', I've missed *that* a whole damn lot," he rasps when we finally pull apart. His hooded eyes and red swollen lips are so enticing I have to fight not to dive in for more. Something about the flash of heat in his gaze tells me he's also struggling not to do. "Before we continue, let's take this somewhere a lot more private. I don't want your daughter tellin' me she caught me neckin' with her mom in her driveway."

My lips curve up. "Wouldn't want that now, would we?"

He chuckles and shakes his head. "Definitely not. So strap yourself in, darlin'."

"I bet you say that to *all* the girls."

Randy's grin widens. "A gentleman never tells, but I will say this. And I want you to let this sink in, Nora McIntyre." He leans in, reaching over and gently gripping the apex of my neck, guaranteeing him all of my focus–although his touch does that, regardless. "There ain't another woman on this earth that I want strapped in my truck, in my arms, and letting me kiss them just the way I like, except you." A gentle gasp catches in my throat, but he keeps going, stroking his thumb over the hinge of my jaw. "You're all I want, and I've wanted you a while now. So sit there and trust me when I say that you're the only woman I see. Just thinkin' of you gets me smiling and hard in the same breath, and that's something that hasn't changed and won't change as far as I'm concerned." He smirks at me as I watch him, unable to breathe, unable to form a coherent thought because I'm stuck on this handsome, strong, wonderful man telling me that I'm everything he wants and needs. *See what I mean, heady!*

Then I stay mute as he lets me go, only then to reach down and grab my seat belt and buckle me in, before lightly gripping my chin and dragging the pad of his thumb down over my bottom lip, gifting me a wicked grin that has me squirming in my seat before he straightens and hooks his truck into reverse.

"Where are you taking me?" I ask when I finally regain the power of speech a few moments later while Randy drives us down the road leading out of town.

He glances my way, shooting me a lopsided, sexy-as-all-get-out smirk. "Now, why would I ruin the surprise?" Oh, so it's like *that,* is it? *Two can play this game, Mr. Barnes.*

I turn my body his way, reaching between us and toying my fingers with the denim covering his knee. "Will I like this surprise?" My voice is light, gentle, but with a flirty edge that the growl rumbling in Randy's chest tells me he didn't miss.

His hand covers mine and after a soft squeeze, he directs my arm back over to my side of the truck's cab. "If ya want me to get us there safe, you're gonna have to stop distractin' me, darlin'."

"Me?"

"Yeah, darlin'. *You.* Any time you touch me, my body gets ideas and right now, I can't do anything about them. So pay a mind to that, yeah?"

I huff out a breath. "You're the one sitting there all swoony and smirky and oozing sexy cowboy vibes out of all of your pores. Maybe *you* should pay a mind to *that*," I say with a little pout.

Randy chuckles, doing that whole sexy one arm on the steering wheel thing that I swear was designed to make every red-blooded woman turn hot. *Then again, every time I'm with Randy my whole body feels like I'm magnetized and on a collision course with him and him alone.*

He laces his fingers with mine, not taking his eyes off the road while lifting my knuckles to his mouth and brushing his lips over them. "OK, darlin'. I'll do that for now."

That's how we stay, driving along a darkened road until Randy turns into what looks like a park and pulls the truck to a stop, shutting the engine off and releasing his seat belt.

"Where are we?" I ask, doing the same and staring out the window, finding myself mesmerized by the dim moonlight shimmering off what looks like water.

"Kinleyville Lake or Makeout Mile, as the *kids* like to say," Randy says with a chuckle.

I arch a brow his way, but can't stop my giggle. "You're showing me your local makeout point?"

"Well, you showed me yours. It's only fair I show you mine," he says, his gaze growing hooded as he rakes his eyes over me, setting me on fire.

My throat goes dry, my nerves sparking, my body trembling, but I somehow stay seated. The air in the truck is thick with lust that's been building for weeks, months—hell, probably even *years*.

"You said...you *needed* to see me?" I say shakily, overwhelmed with just how palpable the pull is between us.

The longer he stares at me, the longer I focus on those perfect bearded lips of his that I've kissed and fantasized about, and the twitching muscle in his jaw that my eyes keep being drawn to. I start to wonder why we're just sitting here and not *doing* something... *anything...*

Then it's like he snaps and in the blink of an eye, Randy's arms are around me as he lays me down on the leather-bench seat and maneuvers his body to cover me, his lips colliding with mine and swallowing my breathy gasp. I drag my fingers through his hair, gripping tight as he kisses me deep and long, his weight deliciously pressing me down, making me feel safe, secure, and *oh* so turned on, it's like I'm coming out of my skin.

"Please," I beg as he buries his face in my neck, kissing, nipping and sucking my skin, causing my back to arch up into him.

"God, you feel so damn good," he rasps, dragging his lips up to mesh with mine again, his tongue doing god's work in my mouth.

"You too. Want more," I pant. "Need... more..." I breathe between kisses.

Randy braces himself up on one arm, his eyes dark in the moonlight streaming in through the windshield as he flattens his palm and runs his hand down over my collarbone and between the valley of my breasts, cupping my aching mound. My breath catches when he rolls his thumb over my straining nipple, the thin material of my shirt and bra doing nothing to dull the connection. As sparks of heat shoot straight between my legs, my hips buck up, pressing hard against his large stiff length, pulsing between us.

"Please, Randy," I beg again.

"Fuck, I can't think straight when you beg me to touch you, darlin'."

I lift my head and touch my lips to his, speaking against them when I say, "Don't think. Just do. We've waited so long for each other."

*That* springs him into action, his mouth slamming back down onto mine, his hand at my breast moving lower, pressing down. He lifts back and our eyes lock, our heavy breaths mingling while his fingers make quick work of the button and zipper of my jeans.

Then I'm moaning against his lips, our tongues tangling as his fingers slide skin to skin down through my wetness, his thumb circling my clit softly, gently, teasingly.

"You're so damn beautiful," he rasps, shifting his weight sideways and cradling my head in his hand as his touch gets fast, firmer, more determined, my core tightening and tingling, my moans growing louder and longer. I don't want this to end, yet I crave the release he's promising me.

"God, you feel so good, so right. So damn hot you're gonna burn me."

"Need you, Randy," I whimper.

"You got me, darlin'. Always." He twists his wrist and trails his fingers lower, toying with my entrance before kissing me soft and slow, easing a thick digit inside of me, connecting us in a way that was meant to be. "Gonna take care of you, Nora." He rolls his hips against my leg as he pushes in and out of me, adding a second finger, filling me, setting my soul on fire, and making my body soar higher and higher. And still we kiss, Randy devouring my mouth with every lash of his tongue and nip of his teeth on my lips.

Then I feel it, the catapulting release barreling toward me like an out of control wave that cannot be stopped. I rip my mouth from his, my muscles tightening, my mind blanking, my vision going white and my nails digging into his scalp so hard they're surely gonna leave a mark as my body clenches tightly around him.

"Randy! Yes. *God!* So good!" I cry out, over and over until I go limp, every bit of tension leaching out of me.

"Fucking gorgeous," Randy murmurs as he peppers my jaw, my chin, my mouth with soft kisses. It's like he can't stop touching me, kissing me, *connecting* with me.

A contented sigh leaves my lips as I run my hands around to cradle his jaw. "Thank you."

Amusement fills his gaze. "Don't thank me for making you feel good when I'm the one bein' given the gift, darlin'."

I quirk a brow. "What about you?" His hard length still presses into my side, but he seems to be ignoring it.

Randy shakes his head. "This wasn't about me."

"It could be?" I say with a flirty grin.

He chuckles and shakes his head again. "Not this time. I'm waitin' for our sleepover since I won't be able to stop once I start with you. Just let me hold you for a spell now, yeah?" And it's that inherent sweetness of his that has my body rallying and trying to recover for another round.

With one last long lingering kiss, he pushes himself up and off me, quickly righting my clothes before helping me back up into a sitting position in his arms.

After sitting there in comfortable silence while I enjoy my post-orgasm haze, he dips his head and kisses me gently before pulling back and staring into my eyes. "I did have something I wanted to talk to you about, though."

My brows brunch together and I scrunch my nose up. "OK..."

"Two things, actually. First, I talked with Leah today."

"Oh no. Please tell me she wasn't rude to you. I'll have a word to her and make her apologize and–" He presses his index finger to my lips to silence me.

"Nothing like that. Well, not really. But I think I got some insight into why she's been actin' out, and I think you should know about it." My head jerks back slightly, a frown pinching my face as he continues, his hand slowly rubbing up and down my thigh. "Somehow Leah has got it into her head that you regret having her. Seems she's created a twisted-up version as to why you protect her so much and why you've moved her away from home–that you don't want her to end up like you, and therefore you see having her as the thing that ruined your life."

I still, my brain getting stuck on his words and how heartbreaking they are. My beautiful, brilliant daughter thinks I *regret* her? *How could she ever think that?!*

"That's not true,' I whisper.

"I know, darlin', and I told Leah as much, too. But with age comes maturity, and from where she's sitting, she says you freaked out when she got a boyfriend, and then you took action to move her away from her home, her friends, her school, all so she wouldn't end up making all the same mistakes you did."

"I did, but it wasn't because I *regret* having her. I can't imagine what my life would be like without her. I don't ever *want* to think about not having her by my side. I just want..." I struggle to find the words.

Randy fans his fingers through my hair and tilts my eyes up to meet his. "You want more for her. More life, more opportunities, more–"

"Time," I say, my voice shaking. "I just want her to take her *time* and enjoy life, smell the roses a little, instead of rushing into responsibility the way I did. If I could have my life over again, I'd do everything the same way, but maybe I'd take a little longer to do it, you know?"

He nods. "That's all any parent ever wants for their children. Hell, It's all any family member or true friend wants for those close to them. It's what I want for you and Leah and your mom, and what I'd hoped for by you movin' here. But I'm thinkin' that maybe a mother-daughter heart to heart could be needed to assuage young Leah about this notion, because knowin' everythin' about you like I do now, I know there's nothin' you wouldn't do for your family. And I know that because you're just like me in that regard."

I sink into his willing arms, sighing in relief and comfort as he wraps me up tight and just holds me, bringing his lips to my temple and pressing them there. "Yeah. Seems we need to sit down and have a no-holds-barred conversation. I don't want her thinking like that when she's the best thing I've ever done with my life. Thanks for telling me, Randy."

I feel his body grow tense. "There's ah... also somethin' else I need to tell you..."

Shifting back, I quirk a brow, wondering what else there could be that could rock my world tonight. My emotions feel like they're yo-yo-ing all over the place, so I'm not sure I can take any more revelations.

Then I realize that Randy looks unsure of himself, and maybe a little nervous. *What on earth could he have to tell me?*

"OK. Hit me with it, Randy. Your body language is getting me worried."

"It's not bad... I'm just not sure how you're gonna take this. But since Leah knows, and I want you to hear it from me, rather than her, I thought it best to explain things now instead of later."

My mind races. Secret Child? Third Nipple? Royalty? *Maybe I read too many romance novels!*

"Do you believe in soulmates, Nora?"

My brows furrow. "I'd like to believe I do."

He nods. "Well, my family–generations of it–believe that there's a spirit, a higher being, that lives within this mountain range. It rewards our kin for living on, working, and protecting her lands." He takes a deep breath, still watching me like a hawk.

"What's the reward?" I ask.

"The Mountain brings our soulmates to us. Our one true love, a mate who's destined to be the other half to our whole–our One."

It takes a while to sink in, but when it does, my whole body jolts with it, a gasp escaping my lips. He runs his hands up my arms, leaving them to rest on my shoulders as his thumbs sweep back and forth over the curve of my throat, leaving a wave of warm tingles in their wake. My heart pounds in my chest as if it's beating just for Randy. I realize that it always seems to go a bit crazy whenever we're together.

"And you think that's *me*?"

"I do." He lightly presses his thumb over the pulse point in my neck. "That's why your heart is racing, just like mine is." He lifts my hand and flattens it over his chest, a forceful thump. thump. thump vibrating against my skin.

"Whoa," I whisper, earning a smile. "Has this happened before?"

Randy nods. "Not to me. But for my brothers and Jasper, and for Miller's brothers before him, and the Coopers at Moose Mountain before that. Every time, they find their soulmate and overcome challenge and adversity before they complete the Mountain's Call and live together in love and eternal happiness for the rest of their days."

I stare up at him, still trying to gather my thoughts.

"Look, I know this is a lot to get your head around, and I've kind of just dumped it all on you. I just felt you should understand what me and my family believe in."

"Thank you," I whisper, appreciating his explanation, even though my mind is still a little muddled.

He reaches up and takes my face in his hands, leaning in to brush his lips against mine before rubbing his thumbs over my cheeks, his gaze roaming over my face intently. "It's getting late. How about I get you home?"

I nod, my mouth void of words as I come to terms with everything Randy just said. *I'm his soulmate and a Mountain Spirit chose me for him? While I like to keep an open mind to most things, I just don't know how to respond to that right now.*

Thankfully Randy Barnes is an understanding man, because the whole drive home, he just holds my hand, keeping our connection but giving me the space I need.

I just hope that a good night's sleep will bring understanding and clarity. *Because Lord knows I need it right now.*

∼

As stealthy as I try to be when I walk back into my house, it's all in vain because I let out a tiny squeak when I find Mom standing at the kitchen counter in her nightgown and robe with a knowing smile playing on her lips and a glass of water in her hand.

"Like mother like daughter, hey?" she says with a whispered laugh.

My cheeks heat but given that I'm a thirty-one-year-old woman, not a sixteen-year-old girl, and Mom's the one that's been openly and enthusiastically encouraging me to 'get a life', I'm not overly embarrassed.

I look at the clock on the wall. "It's not even one in the morning," I reply with a wry grin before I remember everything Randy and I talked about, and my smile falters.

Mom nods. "Touche." She studies me for a bit before her brows scrunch together. "What's wrong?"

Taking a stool opposite her, I meet her eyes. "Do you believe in fate and destiny?"

She stills and I know that wasn't what she expected me to say. "I believe that everything in life happens for a reason, yes. Why's that?"

"Randy believes that I'm his reward–his one true soulmate–brought into his life by a spirit that lives deep within Eagle Mountain."

Mom's eyes widen slightly, but it's in surprise, not shock. There's no disbelief or skepticism in her gaze, either. "Kind of like those books."

"What books?"

"The ones Leah's been reading lately. They're a bunch of romance novels based around here. They're quite fun to read." She smiles to herself before she takes a sip of tea.

"They talk about a Mountain Spirit, do they?"

"They do. It's quite beautiful. The families of the mountains are bound to the Mountain in spirit, and because they don't feel whole living away from their lands, the Mountain Spirit lets out a call that gives their soulmate the inclination to move to the mountain where they reside. When they meet each other, their hearts beat out of control and their blood pumps hot. Oh, and when they touch, there's a surge of energy that makes them feel truly connected."

I step back a little. "I've felt that. It's like I've touched an electric fence, but it doesn't hurt. Like a buzzing under my skin that I only feel when I'm with Randy," I whisper, struggling to believe any of this could be real.

"And what do you think now that Randy has told you about the mountain lore?" she asks, sounding like we're talking about the weather, not some long-lasting, earth-shaking prophecy dictating people's lives and feelings.

I scoff. "I'm kinda rocked, if I'm being honest."

She nods slowly. "I can understand that. But tell me, take a minute and think back to your first reaction when Randy told you about his beliefs, this family legend of his, and tell me... how did you *feel*?"

Opening my mouth to answer, her pointed stare stops me and I pause, taking a deep breath and doing what she said. My first emotion was certainty, like his words had given me the confirmation I needed that this connection we have and the way I feel when I'm with him and how bereft I am *without* him was not just one-sided. Then I let doubt creep in. That's when I kind of internally freaked out and started questioning everything.

I must wear my thoughts on my face because Mom's expression turns from serious to all-knowing. "Someone just figured it all out, didn't she?"

I narrow my eyes. "Surely it can't be real. A *mountain* choosing soulmates and bringing them together? I mean, Randy and I have known each other and worked together for years. Why are we only getting together now?"

"Now, this is something I *can* help you with."

"OK..."

"It wasn't time."

"How do you know?"

She smiles warmly, reaching out and covering my hand with hers before giving me a gentle, reassuring squeeze. "Because, Eleanor, I believe everything happens for a reason, and that means that you and Randy didn't *need* each other in the way you're working toward until now. With Leah, with his ranch, that whole rodeo business you've told me about, all of it. He needs you and you need him. And if the Mountain Spirit is as smart as I think she is–which she must be if she's chosen *you*, my wonderful, intelligent, catch of a daughter, for a good, honest, worthy man like Randy Barnes, then how could you doubt it?"

With one last pat of my hand, Mom straightens and finishes her water before shooting me a smile and wishing me goodnight, leaving me alone in my kitchen, ruminating over her words.

And thank god for mothers, because everything she said was exactly the reassurance I needed to hear. Because there's something to be said about trusting your feelings, *knowing* that something and *someone* who feels as right as my relationship with Randy, is just that.

Right.

## 18

## RANDY

"Hey there, stranger," Kendra calls out to me, smiling as I approach where she and Cass are working with one of their recent rescue horses. "What brings you up this way?"

'This way' is just the top corner of the ranch where Kendra's horse rehabilitation exists. Both she and Jesse live up here, but most of the family gatherings happen at the main ranch house I live in since it's central to everything. I like to keep my nose out of rehabilitation business, so I rarely have a reason to come to Horse Haven unannounced.

"Guess I'm lookin' for a little company and the understandin' of the Mountain's seer," I say, adjusting my hat slightly as I lean on the fencing to make sure the sun isn't shining directly in my eyes.

"This Call thing givin' you the runaround, cousin?" Cass asks, lifting his head from where he's currently trimming the overgrown hoof of an elderly gelding. When Jesse, Cass, and Kendra picked this poor boy up, he could barely walk from how bad it was.

"The Call seems to be doing its thing," I say, a slight smile curving one side of my mouth as I think back to my thoroughly enjoyable tryst with Nora last night. "I've got no complaints there."

Cass and Kendra trade a broad-smiled glance. "Well then, I look forward to another face or two around the dinner table in the near future," he says, sawing the file back and forth while he talks.

"I'm happy you and Nora are getting along, Randy," Kendra adds. "But that means you're up here to talk about the other McIntyre female, the one who's making her feelings about the world and her place in it known."

"You'd be right about that," I say, tipping my hat and smiling. If there's one thing I've learned over the last couple of years watching my family members receive the Call, it's that Kendra will only talk if you give her the space to. As the chosen seer of Eagle Mountain, she's got a deeper connection with the spirit than the rest of us. In her dreams, she communicates and sees the outcome of our relationships before we even know they're starting. But she's sworn to be a guide and never interfere, so the most she can do is listen and advise–in her own sometimes vague, sometimes frustrating way–when we come to a crossroads and can't figure out where to go next. Nevertheless, her knowledge and counsel have never once steered any of us wrong.

"Leah's hurting," Kendra says after a long pause, shaking her head in sympathy. "That much is clear."

I sigh heavily and shove my hands in my pocket. "Yep, she's got it in her head that her mom wishes she'd never been born, which is absolute rubbish. I've never seen a mom sacrifice more for her child than Nora. But I'm thinkin' that's the reason she's fightin' so hard."

"Well, while it may be misguided, Leah inherited that fight from someone," Kendra says with a smile. "And I get a sense that her mom is just as stubborn as she is. So it's gonna take a little time for those two to understand each other and get on the same wavelength."

"She's a teenager, so I'm not sure it's even *possible* to get on the same wavelength, let alone understand it too." I chuckle and lift my gaze to the sky, enjoying the feel of the sun on my skin. "I swear I've never met a woman who's so hell-bent on havin' things her way. Nora would reshape the world with her bare hands if it'd create a better life for her girl."

"An admirable quality," Cass says with a chuckle under his breath. "Pity her teen daughter won't start seein' the strength in that kind of love until she's a mother herself."

I snort and shake my head. "It sure feels that way to me. But I'm hopin' we're not far off breakin' those walls of hers down just enough to get her to stop fightin'."

"And you're hoping that allowing her to work with the horses up here will help?" Kendra asks with her all-knowing smile.

Nodding, I meet her eyes and lift my brow. "You're the only one who might know the outcome of such a thing."

Inhaling a deep lungful of breath, Kendra runs her hand along the neck of the gelding to soothe it when blows out a disgruntled breath. There's a long pause before she turns back to me and I get my answer. "Bring her to me after lunch this Saturday."

"Yeah?" A big grin takes over my face. "So what you're sayin' is that I'm right? That you and the horses might be able to weave your own special kind of magic with young Leah?"

She chuckles and looks at me with sharp eyes. "You're always right, Randy. And I'm not saying that to be facetious. I genuinely feel that you run this family from a place of knowing. You're connected to the Mountain too. You know what's right in your heart, sometimes you just don't know whether to trust it. When it comes to you, dear brother-in-law, it's brain vs heart vs doing right by everyone else before yourself. *Sometimes* you've gotta just go with your gut and let fate lead the way."

With a deeply grateful smile, I tip my hat at her and step back from the fence. "Thanks for the help–and the pep talk, I guess. ."

"I'm here any time," she says with a smile. "Oh, and Randy?"

"Yeah?" I pause and turn back to her.

"Good call stepping in during her interaction with Colton when you did."

Cass's head jerks up as his wide eyes snap between us. "*Why*? What happened?"

I give Kendra a knowing nod before I turn my attention to Cass and wave a dismissive hand. "Nothin' too serious. Just a little flirtin' that I didn't want turnin' into yet *another* reason for Leah to be angry at us all."

"That Colton is a flirt and a half," Cass says with a chuckle. "Reckon he absorbed Sawyer's charm the moment Sawyer wasn't usin' it anymore."

"God help us all then," I say with a laugh.

Kendra makes a face and gets back to work with the horse. "Well, just be careful of that one, Randy," she warns me with a playful smile. "Good to see that fatherly instinct of yours getting a workout because with that one, I get a sense he's got his eye where it doesn't belong. Which is just another valid reason why bringing her up here to work with the horses is a good idea. It'll shift her focus."

My brow perks up at that little sliver of information. "Well then, you've given me hope that we're all headin' along the right path. I'll see you both later," I say, grinning as I walk away, my stride long and purposeful. Leah might still be hurting right now, but once Nora sits her down and clears the air, I have a good feeling that getting the chance to help rehabilitate the horses will be exactly what she needs to forget all about acting out against her mom's rules. And if we're lucky, it'll mean she'll forget all about chasing boys, too.

Seems everything is finally moving in the right direction. Just in time too, because I don't think I can keep waiting to progress my relationship with Nora the way I have been. My body is aching with the need to be with her in more ways than one. I had a taste of her at the lookout, but now I want the whole feast. And the moment she's ready, we'll be making that promised sleepover a reality. Not that there'll be much sleeping involved, not if I have anything to do about it.

## 19

## NORA

After picking up Leah early from the ranch, I knock on her bedroom door, waiting for her to say, "come in," before stepping inside and smiling at her, all cleaned up and a hoodie and leggings lying on her bed.

"Hey, sweetheart. I was wondering if we could have a chat," I say gently, taking in the suspicious expression that appears on her beautiful face. She's the perfect mix of me and her father, and at first, I thought that would make his decision not to be involved in her life a lot harder for me to get over. But the moment she was placed in my arms, all puffy-faced and screaming to the heavens, all of that was forgotten. It was love at first sight between me and my baby girl, and that feeling has just continued to grow and deepen as we've both matured, the two of us growing up side by side as it turned out.

Just the thought that she'd ever think I'd regret that–regret *her*–breaks my heart.

There's no missing the tensing of my daughter's shoulders as she sits up and leans against her headboard. I cross the room and sit down on her bed, smiling at her as I look down at a half-read copy of an Aster Hollingsworth cowboy romance. I recognize the title because after Mom told me about the books the other night, I made a point of looking up the author and *may* have downloaded the first title onto my e-reader. I mean, if these books give me some insight into the Mountain's Call and the Barnes family beliefs, then I'd be stupid not to do a little research. *Well, that's what I tell myself when buying the next book in the series as soon as I finish the last one, anyway.*

"Thought you were going out tonight." There's no missing the slight snark in her voice, but I ignore it and forge on. *She's not the only stubborn McIntyre woman in the room.*

I nod, then look down at the paperback on the bed. "Enjoying the book?"

She shrugs, her eyes drifting down to it. "It's OK."

Smiling, I chuckle. "Must be good if you're moving through the series. Do they have them all at Kinleyville Library?"

Her gaze widens with surprise. "How did you know I'd been going there?"

"It's my job to know, sweetheart. That's what moms do." She narrows her eyes suspiciously. "*And* Nanny told me." She huffs out a breath.

"Figures." We're both quiet for a while. "Have you read them too?"

"I may be a little addicted to them now. I started when Nanny told me about them, and I haven't been able to stop."

Leah regards me for a spell, then nods before giving me an unexpected gift. "They give me hope," she confesses, and my heart swells because *this*, this right here, is my gorgeous little girl coming to the forefront. And I couldn't have asked for a better segue.

I reach out and give her leg a gentle squeeze. "Well, we all need a bit of that in our lives now and then, don't we?"

Seeing her shoulders relax just a little, I decide it's high time to say what I need to say. "I wanted to talk to you about something Randy said to me..."

Her back goes ramrod straight on the bed. "I've been behaving myself!" she says, jumping straight into defensive mode.

"Hey, I know. It's nothing to do with your work at the ranch, OK?" She relaxes a little and I press on. "It's more about me being worried that you think I regret having you." Leah's eyes widen and her lips part, but she doesn't say a word, so I press on. "I really hope I haven't ever made you feel that way, sweetheart, because nothing could be further from the truth. I was lost when I fell pregnant with you, and I can't even explain why. I think it was because Mom was working a lot to provide for me, and I started developing and catching attention from the cute boys at school, and I liked it." I dip my head a little and drop my voice to a whisper. "Especially the bad boys."

Leah's lips twitch a little before she catches herself and I give myself an internal fist pump. *Keep going, Nora.*

"So when your father asked me to hang out with him and his friends, I was flattered. I mean, I was a freshman, and they were sophomores. Yeah, I liked the attention. I liked him and his friends, and whenever we went out, we'd have fun, you know? And although I didn't like sneaking out and disobeying Nanny, it was nice. Thrilling, even."

"If you're about to tell me about you losing your v-card and getting pregnant with me, can we skip that part? Like *all together* because, eww." She scrunches her nose up, making me snort, but I nod in agreement.

"Well, obviously I found out I was pregnant, and I told Nanny, but something changed in me after that. It was like I had a purpose, a reason to turn my life around, and that, sweetheart, was you. Then you were born and from the very second I laid eyes on you, I *knew* that I'd move heaven and earth, even mountains, just to keep you safe and well and make sure you thrived."

She starts worrying her bottom lip between her teeth, but I don't miss the almost imperceptible nod to continue.

"So when you started acting out, yes, I freaked out because I knew what it was like, and my brain jumped to worst-case scenarios if you kept down the path you seemed determined to go down in Timber Falls." Leah's brows furrow at that but I press on. "The thing is, I may react quickly, and sometimes without any warning–"

"Like moving us to a whole new *town*," she says in a typical teenage 'duh' tone.

"Yep. Like getting scared out of my brain when I get a call that my sixteen-year-old daughter is being held at a *police* station hours and hours away from home with her boyfriend who I can see—just like what happened to me—is leading her astray."

A resigned sigh escapes her lips. "Yeah. I get that." Part of me wants to jump up in the air and yell *'yahoo',* because if I'm not mistaken, Leah and I have just had a breakthrough.

"But did you have to just *move* us? I mean, I like it here and all, but it's not *home*."

I rub my hand over her knee. "Yeah, sweetheart. I did. Because I was trying to protect you. From heartache. From being forced to grow up too quickly. From losing the heart of who *you* are because you're trying to impress a boy... There isn't anything I wouldn't do for you and your grandmother. Absolutely nothing, baby. I'd walk over hot coals, scale mountains, and slay dragons for you if it means you're safe, happy, and the world stays your oyster."

She scrunches her nose up at that, a smile playing on her lips. "Well, you don't have to go *that* far. I mean, I doubt there are any *dragons* in Kinleyville."

I laugh and shake my head. "No, just match-making Mountain Spirits apparently."

"You *know* about that?" she gasps. "It's crazy, right? I mean. Randy totally believes in it and didn't seem to like me questioning it."

"Yeah. He told me about it the other night and it's taken a few days for me to wrap my head around it, but a lot of what he said and a lot of the things I've been feeling for Randy make a lot of sense now."

She tilts her head as if to study me. "Like what?"

"You didn't wanna talk about me losing my v-card, and you wanna talk about *this*?" I quirk a brow, earning rolled eyes and a frustrated sigh.

"Well, *duh*! This is like fiction becoming real life, and who *wouldn't* want that? Like reading in Aster's books about the instant connection between the hero and their Ones? That's goals right there. So if you're feeling anything like that with Randy, of course I wanna know." She leans forward. "Like I don't wanna know about any of the sex stuff because *eww*, but the whole feeling like you're whole when you're together, physically missing him when you're apart, the heart racing, the blood pumping, all of that... do you feel any of it?"

I nod, unable to stop the smile growing on my face. "Yeah, I do. I just didn't put any of it together until Randy said something and then I read the books."

"It's kinda cool, right?" My sweet girl is *totally* a closet romantic. Maybe Eagle Mountain works a bit of magic in all ways, not just for the protectors of the land and their soulmates. Maybe it works for the residents of the town too.

Because of all the things I thought would happen with this little conversation between me and my daughter, I didn't expect it to turn into a *bonding* moment, that's for sure.

"What I want to make sure you know, deep down in your soul, is that I love you, and there has never been a single day since the moment you were born that I've ever not been thankful to have been given the gift of you, OK? I just want you to have anything and everything you could ever want in life, and if that means grounding you, cussing you out to make you see reason, or *yes*, moving towns to start afresh– whatever it takes, whatever I have to do, I'm gonna do it, Leah. Because my life begins and ends with you and your grandmother. That's it."

"OK." That's all she says. Here I am pouring my heart and soul out to my flesh and blood and she sums up everything with a simple 'OK.' "What about Randy? Aren't you going out there tonight?"

"He's becoming important to me, yes."

She nods. "OK."

*Ugh, how can teenage speak can be so infuriating and hilarious all at the same time?*

"That's it?" I ask. "Just *OK*?"

"Yep." She smirks, like she knows what she's doing to me right now.

"No opinion about me dating Randy or anything?"

"Nope," she replies, accentuating the P as she reaches down to pick up her book.

I stand, a little bit lost and confused as to what to do now. I mean, that was *far* too easy and straightforward... right?

"Well, I guess I better get ready to go then."

"Sounds good, Mom," she says, snuggling back down into her bed and burying her nose in her book, making my heart melt that little more.

I reach the door and stop, turning back to look at her again. "See you tomorrow?"

"Yep."

"And you'll stay in tonight? No sneaking out?" It hasn't been a problem since we moved, but old habits die hard I suppose.

Leah rolls her eyes. "No, Mom. It's not like there's anything to *do* in this town, anyway. Besides, I'm just getting to the good part." She waves her book in the air, making me smile. "And Nanny already said she'd drop me off at the ranch tomorrow morning, so don't worry about coming home."

I stare dumbfounded as she effectively dismisses me, still in a daze as I walk down to the kitchen where Mom is prepping vegetables for dinner.

"You look a bit lost there, Eleanor. Did it go OK?"

I stare at Mom, wondering if Leah's bedroom is a vortex to another universe or something.

"Yeah. Too well. When did she grow up?"

Mom chuckles and shakes her head. "You're asking *me* that question when I wonder that myself every time I look at the *both* of you."

"I think we did the right thing moving here," I say, moving close to my mom and dropping a kiss on the top of her head.

"Yeah. Me too," she says, wishing me a 'fun evening' while I grab my coat and bag in and head out, driving to the ranch where Randy is cooking me dinner, and I'm hoping we might *finally* get a chance to have that grown-up sleepover we've been planning for so long…

## 20

## RANDY

With pots boiling over and timers going off left, right and center, I'm starting to wish I'd taken Ellie-Mae up on her offer to cook something I can finish off in the oven. But no, being the stubborn ass that I am, I insisted on cooking this whole thing from scratch, and now...well, let's just say it looks like my kitchen just exploded.

I feel like a bumbling fool.

The timer goes off again, and I turn it off in a flurry of annoyance before going to check on my potatoes. I poke them with a fork and determine that they're not quite done yet. "Fucking hell," I mutter under my breath, watching for headlights through the open door from the corner of my eye so I don't miss Nora's arrival.

Throughout the entirety of today, I've been so eager to see her that I wanted to speed up time.

But right now, in the midst of my very poor juggling act, I'm willing it to slow down. She's going to walk in here and think she's got me all wrong, and I'm not the capable man she thought I was. Inviting her here and cooking for her is about her seeing me in my element, getting a glimpse of what a real relationship with me would be like. And I'm pretty sure there isn't anything good about seeing me in a frilly apron in a kitchen with food splattered from one end of the counter to the other. This is a disaster.

Hearing the crunching of gravel as a car pulls up outside, I peek out the door and see Nora's sedan coming to a stop next to my truck. "She's early. Shit." With a rocket under my ass, I grab the oven mitts from their hook on the wall before rushing to pull the beef out. My potatoes are still a little crunchy at the center, and I have no idea how much longer I need to cook them for to fix that, but hopefully they'll be fine with some gravy over top of them. I just hope Nora doesn't mind lumps...

Setting the roast brisket on the cutting board, I quickly carve—well, hack—it up, trying to get dinner to some semblance of 'ready' before Nora walks in. I hear her footsteps on the porch, so I set my knife to the side and flick off the burners, wiping my hands on my apron as she knocks, and I make a beeline for the door to greet her.

"Coming," I call out.

*Wait. My apron.*

Frantic, I pull at the somehow-twisted tie and look around for a place to stash it. But the damn thing won't unknot and I'm huffing, puffing and starting to sweat just trying to angle my hands behind my back to get it undone. *Fuck.*

Suddenly, the door opens and Nora walks in. We both freeze as she looks at me with a furrowed brow. "Ahh...you did say 'come in', right?"

"Erm..." I'm stuck hunched over, my hands twisted behind my back, all while wearing a floral apron with pink frills over the top of my good jeans and a clean button up. I can't think of a worse way to make a first-official-date impression right now.

"Killer look," she says, and I snap out of my embarrassment when she approaches and kisses me on the cheek. "I thought you were supposed to be cooking dinner, not wearing it...What happened here?"

"Dinner kind of got away from me a little. Figured I'd pre-warn you so you have time to lower your expectations before we sit down to eat," I say, rubbing at my neck and trying not to look her in the eye for fear she'll be disgusted with my lack of culinary skills. This was supposed to be a romantic evening for just the two of us, but already, it's turning out less than expected.

"Well, it smells good. So that's a start." She looks up at me before reaching out to swipe her finger through a splatter of gravy on the front of my apron and tastes it. "Tastes OK too."

"Fuck, I love you," I blurt without thinking, a smile curving my mouth as I take in her gorgeous, upturned face. The moment I realize what I've said, my eyes bug out, and I don't even give her a chance to respond before I start blabbering and kicking myself internally all over again. "Anyway, the food's all ready. Just give me a minute to wash up and I'll serve it to you."

"OK," she gets in, just before I rush down the hall and close myself into the bathroom. Muttering and cussing myself out as I splash some water over my face and finally get myself free of the blasted apron.

"Be cool, Randy. You're actin' like a bumbling virgin on prom night who's never had a date in his life," I say to my dripping wet reflection before I swipe a towel across my face, taking a deep breath to clear my mind, then stepping down the hall to head back out to Nora.

"You'll have to excuse the crunchiness," I say as we sit across from each other at the dinner table. "Ellie-Mae does most of the cookin' around here."

"It's OK," she says, chewing slowly, her eyes glowing from the light of the small candle I placed in the table setting, along with a jar of wildflowers I collected during my rounds on the ranch today. "Crunchy potatoes with chewy gravy creates an interesting texture profile. You might be onto something here." She grins up at me, and I'm caught between reacting defensively and hugging her for being so damn understanding and for putting this goop in her mouth without complaint.

"Maybe I should stick to making stuff I know, like chili and tacos. I can bang those out all day long. "

"Don't be so hard on yourself. The beef is perfect."

"OK. I'm going to take that one compliment, but the rest is terrible and I'm begging you to quit eatin' it," I say, finally letting myself smile back at her.

"But it's delicious," she teases, popping another forkful in her mouth and smiling at me as she makes a show of chewing it exaggeratedly.

"Oh, my god. Stop." I laugh. "We'll just call it quits here and move on to dessert."

With an amused smile, she lowers her fork and wipes her mouth with a napkin as I reach across the table to take her plate away. But before I can, she places her hand on my wrist, her green/blue eyes meeting mine with a hint of mischief in them.

"Can I make a confession, Randy?"

"Of course."

"As much as I appreciate the gesture and the sentiment behind you cooking me dinner. It wasn't your *food* I came here for tonight. I came for you."

Forgetting all about the clearing of *anything*, I take a quick stride around the table and gather her into my arms, running my nose alongside hers as I just breathe in her closeness. "Then I think I should make a confession, too."

"Yeah?" she whispers, sliding her arms up over my shoulders, fingers skirting around the collar of my shirt.

"What I said to you before? I meant it. Every word," I murmur, watching closely as her gaze softens and her pulse quickens alongside mine. "It may be fast, but to me it's not fast enough, because I've wasted more than enough time not sharin' my feelings with you, darlin'. And–"

She presses her index finger against my lips. "I'm not hungry for dessert anymore, Randy," she says, the hand between us dropping away just before I let out a rumble in agreement and bring my mouth to hers, kissing her until the only thing I can feel or remember is the sense of being here with her—my one true mate.

## 21

## NORA

Randy kisses me the whole time he carries me out of the kitchen and down the hall. Then I'm kissing him as he steps inside his bedroom and kicks the door shut.

Lowering me slowly down his body until my feet touch the ground, I barely need nor care to breathe when I see the man's darkened gaze raking over me.

"You. here. In my house. My arms. My bedroom." His voice is full of so much wonder. He crowds me against the door, his body heat scorching me as my heart thumps hard against my ribs. "Dreamed of this moment, darlin'."

"Me too."

He shakes his head, his eyes hooded and so damn hot I worry I'm about to combust in the doorway before I even get to see him naked. "Gonna make you mine, Nora. Claim every inch of you. Show you how much I love you with my body"—he presses me into the door with his hips, his hard length standing proud between us—"Take you with my lips, my tongue, my hands..." His hands drag up my sides, skimming my breasts as he softly, slowly, teasingly licks into my mouth, making me whimper. When he moves his thick, jean-clad thigh between my legs and presses against my core, something snaps inside me.

"Please," I beg before gripping his face in my fingers and kissing him back, harder, deeper, messier and full of some much need and want and craving that I lose myself in him, not even realizing Randy has lifted me and crossed the room until I drop back onto the bed and bounce against the mattress.

I watch him strip off his shirt and shuck down his jeans until he's standing in front of me in just his boxers, stuck in a stupor and potentially drooling while I watch his strip show. With a mind of their own, my fingers go to the buttons on my shirt, needing and wanting to get skin-on-skin with this man as soon as possible.

Randy's lips tip up on the side as he shakes his head and stalks toward me on the bed. "Been dreamin' about stripping you naked for years now, Nora. Don't take that away from me when we're so close that I can smell what I do to you."

"Damn, you could make me climax with your words alone, Randy. Do you know that?"

He puts a knee to the mattress between my feet and slowly climbs up my body, his hands going to my shirt and bra first before dropping to my jeans, making quick work of removing everything and dragging the denim down my legs until I'm lying there in just my black lace underwear.

He drags his lips down my legs before nuzzling behind my knee and slowly trailing his tongue up my inner thigh, every part of me anticipating and begging him to keep going where I want him most. But with a satisfied chuckle, he runs over my hip and in, circling my navel before gliding his body up and claiming my lips with his again. Everywhere he touches or kisses me, he leaves a brand on my heart in his wake. Nothing and no one has ever made me feel the way Randy Barnes does. It's like we were always meant to be together, to be here…

Our tongues wrestle, our hands roam, his grunts and my moans filling the air as we take our fill. Randy's palm cups my breast over my shirt, and then it's both of us fighting to rid each other of the last semblance of clothing separating us.

"So beautiful, Nora," he murmurs, bracing himself over me, his eyes roaming my face, his knuckles dragging ever so gently down my cheek, my collarbone, and down between the valley of my chest, tracing my sternum and making me tremble. My heart doesn't know what the hell it's doing now. All I know is that it beats for this man, this moment...

I tilt my head and grin up at him. "You look like a kid in a candy shop, Randy Barnes."

He chuckles before dipping down and wraps his lips around one of my stiff peaks, swirling his tongue before moving to pay the same attention to the other side. My back arches up off the bed, the feelings he's eliciting so powerful, so amazing.

"Randy..." I moan, tangling my fingers through his hair, loving the feel of his weight on me, his skin hot against mine, his mouth, teeth, and tongue exploring everywhere they can reach as he slowly, methodically tastes every inch of me he can reach, moving lower.

Dipping his fingers under the waist of my underwear, he looks up and quirks a brow, my breaths coming in heaving desperate pants now, needing him to do something, anything, to put his mouth back on me somewhere... *anywhere!*

I nod a little too enthusiastically, earning a chuckle and a soft pressed kiss against my pelvic bone as he drags the black lace down my legs and away, baring me to him. Randy's dark eyes flare with heat and passion, so intense I squirm under his gaze, every ion of my being drawn to this handsome man.

"Need to taste you, Nora. Need to feel you on my tongue. You're mine, just as I am yours. Just as we were always meant to be." His words make my pulse spike, my stomach flip, and my soul sigh like it's finally found its home.

Then his wide shoulders are spreading me open for him, his gaze never leaving me as he licks his lips and dips his head.

"Please," I pant, my fingers fisting the covers beneath me.

My heart races and my eyes flutter shut as he blows a slow, hot breath over my soaked seam. A desperate cry escapes me when he dives in tongue first, swiping over my clit, soft at first, then firmer, more determined. He circles the nub with the tip before softly sucking the swollen bundle of nerves between his lips, my back bowing off the mattress as a loud cry escapes me.

His big hands frame my hips and rock me against him as he devours me, licking, tasting, consuming me whole while sliding the tip of his tongue back and forth. Randy's rumbling groans and rough growls send lightning bolts of lust ping-ponging from the top of my head to the tip of my toes, centering in my core as the spring coiled there gets tighter and tighter.

I clench my thighs against his shoulders, fearing I'll explode into a million pieces and welcoming the pleasure this amazing man is drawing out of me. My hips start to move, grinding against him and driving him crazy. I ride his lips and tongue, my grip on his hair tightening as I chase the tingling climax he's working to give me.

Proving he's an intuitive lover, he senses my need for climax and shifts his hand between my legs, gliding his fingers to my drenched entrance, stroking once, then twice before easing them into me, filling me. Everything I've ever known and wondered about clicking into place in that very miraculous instant when I clench around him, sucking him in and not letting go as my mind goes blank, my vision turns white, and I cry out his name over and over.

"Randy. Oh, my god. Yes!" I shout, grateful that we're the only ones in the house as wave after wave of ecstasy roll over me.

He slowly brings me back down from my incredible high, his voice rough as he murmurs 'I love you,' between peppered kisses all over my sex, my hips, my stomach, my breasts, trailing up until his face hovers over mine and his lips are a whisper's breath away.

Needing to make him feel just as good as he's made me, I tangle one hand in his brown locks, holding his mouth against mine as I nip and lick and kiss him deeply. My other hand snakes between us, pushing his boxers down and wrapping my fingers around his shaft as much as I can hold. Squeezing and stroking, dragging my hand from the base right to the tip and back again, loving the feel of the weight of him in my palm.

"You feel so good, Randy," I murmur against his lips, loving the gasps and stuttered breaths coming out of the man that's come to mean everything to me. He thrusts into my hand, his cock swelling and throbbing in my hold.

"Fuck, darlin'. You keep doing that and this'll be over before it's even begun." He lifts his head and shifts out of my hold, his lips curling when I pout at the loss.

With his lips against mine, he rocks my world and almost makes me come again with what he says next. "I want to be inside you, Nora. This is when I make you mine forever. Nothing between us, nothing to stop us, just you and me forever. Yeah?"

I nod as tears of happiness fill my eyes.

He grips the base of his hard length, squeezing it tight as he positions himself where we both want him to be. One hand comes to the side of my head, the other between us as he circles his cockhead around my clit.

There's no mistaking the delicious wave of pleasure that fills every fiber of my being when Randy presses his forehead to mine, our gazes locked together so we're all the other can see and feel. Then, it's like something snaps between us. He thrusts up and I shift forward, our hips drawn together like magnets as he buries himself deep inside me, the sound of his low, satisfied growl filling the air and vibrating over my skin. But that's not the most overwhelming feeling in a sea of overwhelming feelings, because in that moment, Randy on me, in me, all around me, I'm filled with a sense of absolute completeness the likes of which I've never felt before.

Needing to kiss him like he's the very air I need to breathe, I grip his jaw and stare deep into those beautiful soulful eyes I know I'm meant to lose myself in for the rest of my days.

"I love you too, Randy. Please make me yours."

## 22

## RANDY

Buried inside her deliciously slick heat, I know I've just found my one true addiction. She feels like heaven as she sucks me in and squeezes me tight, my entire body threatening to explode with the euphoria that can only come from finally being complete.

Nothing has ever felt this good.

Threading my fingers with hers, I lift her hands above her head and thrust. Thrust. Thrust.

Her body jolts with the force of my movement, breasts swaying, mouth open and gasping. The sight of her beneath me has me thinking all kinds of weird and wonderful long-term things. But even though we've finally taken this step to fully join and answer the Mountain's Call, I know our journey is nowhere near complete.

"So good, Randy. I'm so full," she gasps, her fingers pressing into my skin, nails breaking the surface.

"Fuck, darlin'. You're so tight. So perfect for me," I hiss through my teeth, her sweet moans driving me insane as I quicken my pace to match her tilting hips, rising to meet me thrust for thrust. "I need more of you."

"More?"

"Wanna be deeper. As far as I can go." Shifting back, I place my hands on her hips, lifting her slightly and pummeling into her faster and harder. She cries out, her back arching, thrusting her perfect breasts toward me, making my mouth water.

"Holy shit! Yes! Randy!" She thrashes her head from side to side, a guttural moan escaping her as her insides grip tighter around my cock and threaten to unman me.

"Fuck, Nora. You're gonna milk me dry."

"More. Please."

Lifting her a little higher, I thruster faster, harder, deeper.

"Oh, Randy!" Her words come out as high-pitched cries and I pump, pump, pump, finding stamina I never thought I was capable of. Sweat drips down my back and my balls beg for release, but this feels too good, and I've waited for too long.

"Not yet, darlin'. Hold on for me."

"Fuck, Randy! Please!"

Throwing her leg over my shoulder, I lift her even higher, angling myself inside her even deeper, the length of my dick grinding along her g-spot and sending her shrieking and clawing at the sheets as she lets out an almighty howl.

"Raaaandy!" Her release hits her, her body jolting as the orgasm takes hold of her movement. But I keep fucking going, seeming unable to stop. I'm by no means a young man, anymore, but it's like I can't get enough of this woman and her body, her soul is calling to mine like no one ever has, and it's like I have this desperate need to make her come so hard she screams.

"Fuck, Nora, you're like a vice. So fucking good," I grunt, keeping her riding the high of that wave for as long as I possibly can.

"Ran-dy!" Animalistic noises come out of her as her hands wrap around my wrists and her entire body goes rigid, yet another orgasm hitting her and stealing away her breath.

The look of pure ecstasy on her face robs me of the last vestiges of my restraint, and I yell out my release, pouring myself inside of her over and over again as if my body is no longer under my control. "Fuck me! Holy hell! Nora! You're so fuckin' amazin'."

"Oh god. I could barely breathe through that last one," Nora gasps as I collapse on the bed beside her.

"I could barely move you were squeezin' me so tight." I let out a chuckle as I wrap my arms around her and pull her into my arms. "That was the best, mind-bending, life-altering sex of my life, so if you think you're gonna get away from me now, you've got no chance, Nora McIntyre. I'll handcuff you to me if I have to."

Giggling, Nora rolls in close to my chest and rakes her fingers through the underside of my beard. "I'm going to take that as an amazing compliment. And I'm not sure you'll have to keep me handcuffed if you keep loving on me like that. But if we're sharing secrets—it was the best mind-bending, life-altering sex I've ever had too. That Call is really something, huh?"

"Yeah," I rasp, my heart still thumping hard in my chest. Who needs a cardio check-up when you can just have sex like that to remind you that you're still alive and kicking? "I reckon the mountain might know what she's doing, even if she did take her sweet ass time decidin' it was my turn."

"Maybe we should try it one more time," she says as she walks her hand down my chest toward my still-ready dick. "You know, just to be sure..."

"I'm game if you are," I say, quirking my brow as she gives me a husky laugh before she kisses her way down my torso and gives me a treat I'll never forget...

## 23

## NORA

"Good mornin', love birds," Ellie-Mae says in her twinkly twang as Randy and I walk hand in hand into the kitchen. "I'd ask how last night went, but if the state of this kitchen when I walked in was anything to go by, I already know the answer to that." She flashes us a bright smile from where she stands at the stove preparing breakfast. "I'm guessin' you both need some stomach-stickin' breakfast this morning?" I feel my cheeks heat, but the warm smile on Randy's sister's lips goes a long way to lessen my embarrassment. I mean, I'm a thirty-one-year-old woman with a teenage daughter. It's not like the world doesn't know I've had sex before. But even still...

"Hey, now, Ellie-Mae. That's no way to treat a house guest, is it? And I apologize for the mess I left in here. You could probably tell that me cookin' dinner ended in disaster." Despite the chastising words, there's no real malice in Randy's tone toward his sister. If anything, there's a little humor laced in there. "Thank god you thought to leave some snacks in the refrigerator, though." He leads me over to where Ellie is stirring a pot and kisses her cheek. "You're right about needing some of that cowboy brew of yours, though. My love and I could use a little liquid gold to get through the day."

My eyes bug out at that last comment. *My love...* Gosh, that's both weird and surreal now that I know it's true. Randy and I love each other, and it's in a way that it's never going to wane either. It's like a tangible thing that tethers us together. Mountain's Call or not, I have to hope that Randy and I would've always gotten to this point. The fact I'm sore and achy in the best possible way after a night of love-making confirms it. This man and I are a match made in mountain heaven.

"Here you both go," Ellie says, making quick work of filling two travel cups and handing them to us. "And it's a good thing y'all are already dressed because Kendra called and Nora's mom and Leah are on their way. That's why I'm here. I'm making breakfast burritos to go for y'all. Apparently, you have plans at the Horse Haven today?" The lilt in her voice at the end has me thinking she's both curious and confused. *You and me both, Ellie.*

My head jerks back just as Randy's drops forward. "Wait... how does Kendra know Mom and Leah are on their way? Did she see their car or something?"

Ellie quirks a brow at Randy. "Yeah, Randy. How *does* Kendra know?"

"Thanks for the coffee, sis," he mutters as he reaches down and laces his fingers with mine. "We'll go wait for Leah and Beverly outside."

"All right. But don't go far. I'm almost done with your food." Ellie says as she returns to the stove. Randy leads me to where our boots and his hat are by the back door.

Once we're outside, I look up at him. "So, Kendra?"

He gestures to a picnic table and wooden benches set up outside the ranch house, taking a seat next to me. "Kendra has a deeper connection with the Mountain Spirit than the rest of us. When she and Jesse were goin' through their own Call, it came about that the spirit communicates with her in her dreams. At first, she thought she was crazy and losing her mind a bit, but once we found out what was happening, we called in Tim–aka Gandalf, the Seer from Bear Mountain—and also Aster Hollingworth who has seeing abilities of her own. They figured it out, and now Kendra's a lot more at ease with her role."

I gasp. "You mean Aster's books are about these mountains and your family?"

Randy's eyes widen. "You read romance novels, darlin'?"

"All three of us do. Leah started Aster's first book, then Mom told me, and now we're all hooked on them." I shake my head. "I can't believe you know her. She's famous!"

He chuckles. "She's not famous to us. She's just another member of our mountain family. It was her and her husband, Gray, who reignited the spirit over at Moose Mountain. After all the Cooper brothers heard the Call and met their soulmates, it jumped over to Bear Mountain to the founding brothers of the Homestead up there."

"That's amazing. So Kendra can see the future, too?" I ask, taking a sip from my mug and groaning at how good—and strong—the coffee is.

"She can see the outcome of our relationships before we even know they're starting. But she's sworn to be a guide, and she never interferes. She's all about preserving the journey and making sure everyone going through the Call gets exactly what they need from the experience."

"What do you mean? She's like the Mountain's resident guidance counselor?" I ask with a confused frown.

Randy chuckles and throws his arm over my shoulder, pulling me into his warmth. "The most she can do is listen and advise us when we seek her guidance."

"OK... so how does that have anything to do with Horse Haven and her knowing Leah and Mom are coming?"

"I was gonna talk to you about that, actually, but I got a little waylaid last night."

"Well, I got waylaid..." I say with a cheeky grin, earning me a growl against my lips as Randy takes my mouth hard and deep and oh so delicious.

"Unless you want us to get caught in a compromisin' position by your mom and daughter, and probably some of my brothers and cousins too, you best not be reminding me about how much I want to waylay you again, yeah?"

I smirk against his mouth, our eyes locked together. "You can remind me again later if you want."

"Fuck," he grunts, reaching down to adjust himself. "You've got my body thinking I'm thirty again."

Shrugging, I straighten and take another glug from my mug. "Well, they do say you're only as old as the woman you're feeling…"

Randy chuckles and shakes his head at me. "Too true."

"So Kendra, the Horse Haven… Leah?"

"Oh yeah. You distracted me with your kissable lips and tempting thoughts. I wanted to see what you thought of me suggestin' to Leah that she spend some time with Kendra up at the Horse Haven. That's her rehabilitation ranch next to ours."

"I remember that. Jesse bought the property for her a few years back and you guys incorporated it with the ranch, but it's run as a separate not-for-profit, right?"

"Yes, ma'am. Workin' side by side with Leah, I've noticed more than once that she has a real affinity for horses, and I think that seeing the good work that Kendra does with the orphaned and rehomed animals she has over there might spark something in her, maybe even give her thoughts about a future career on the land. She's got a real knack for it when she's not scowlin' and poutin' and flirtin' with Colton."

Now that gets my attention. "Flirtin' with *Colton*? How old is *he*?"

"Hey. It's all in hand, darlin'. I caught them talkin', picked up on the vibe, and shut that down, makin' my thoughts on the matter as clear as can be. He may be a teenager himself, but he's still too old for her for my likin', and I–" He stops talking, realizing that I'm gazing up at him like he's just opened up the window to my soul to let the sunshine in. "Nora?"

"You just sounded like a father figure just then."

"Well, she's your daughter, and I intend to make you mine, darlin'. So there's no just about it. Listen to me and let it sink in. I have every intention of being in your life for a long time. All of your lives, you, Leah, and your mom. You're family now, just as much as my brothers, cousins, sister, and all their kin are. In return, I hope you see them as yours as well."

"I love you. Do you know that?"

"I do. And it makes me feel ten feet tall and bulletproof." I lean forward and kiss him this time, soft and slow, pouring my feelings into our connection so they don't overflow out of me.

"So Leah and horses, huh?"

"Yeah. She's got a soft heart and a gentle soul under all that teenage angst and emotional armor."

"Yeah, she does. And yes, I think we should see whether it's something she's interested in."

He covers my hand and gives it a squeeze before looking up at the driveway. "Good, because here comes your mom's car. "

## 24

## RANDY

After sharing breakfast burritos with Leah and Nora's mom, Beverly, she heads home while Nora and I take Leah up to Horse Haven to see Kendra. As expected, Leah is beyond excited to be spending the entire day up there, so when Nora and I get back into the Gator, we head back to the ranch house with a smile on our face and hope in our hearts.

"I really think Leah is coming good," Nora says with a happy sigh as we bump along the back roads that join properties.

"Yeah?" I turn and flash her a grin, enjoying the gentle flush in her cheeks and the bright shine in her eyes I like to think I've played a part in putting there. "I kinda think so, too. Amazin' what a little responsibility and fresh air can do for a young person."

"She has direction now." Reaching out, she places her hand on my thigh. "Thank you, Randy. From the bottom of my heart. For all you've done, and all you keep promising to do. I don't think I could have found a better man to invite into our lives than you. I trust you completely."

My heart swells about twice its size inside my chest as I cover her hand with mine, then lift it to kiss the back of her knuckles. Having a family of my own is something I've wished for more often than not for a good twenty years now. And even though Leah might not be my blood, to be given the chance to finally, *finally* do right by a child and an amazing woman like Nora? Well, that's more than I could hope for.

"We're gonna be a family, baby," I tell her with quiet conviction. "You, me, Leah, and even your mom. I'm gonna make it perfect for all of you."

She turns and beams at me, a pretty blush still staining her cheeks. "I believe you. There's absolutely no doubt in my mind about this—about *us*—Randy. I love you. You're my soulmate, my *One*, just as much as I'm yours. Some might say you're stuck with me now."

I chuckle, my lips tugging up into a smirk. "Sounds perfect to me, darlin'. Cause I'm not lettin' you go now, anyway."

We bump along in silence for a bit, the only sound the steady hum of the Gator and my mind playing out possible scenarios for our future—all of them happy.

"I'm guessing that there's no rest for the wicked, and you have to do some work today?" Nora asks as I make the final turn and bring us to a stop outside the main barn.

"Nope," I say with a grin, taking off my Stetson as I turn toward her. "Got the boys coverin' for me. My schedule is clear. I'm all yours for the day."

A sexy smile that has my heart thumping and my body reacting spreads across her face. "Well then, I suppose I should check to make sure my schedule is clear." She pulls her cell from her pocket and makes a show of tapping at the screen and thinking hard. "Hmm. It's a Sunday... so that means... Hmmm. Just as I thought. Nothing. I'm all yours." She giggles, then turns a brilliant smile my way, moving to shut off her phone before pausing and doing a double-take. "Oh shit. I knew it would be a mistake opening my email."

"What?" I knit my brow and watch her with concern as she lifts her eyes to mine.

"I've been CC'd on an email from your lawyer. Seems the rodeo wants to pursue their claim over Bruiser in the courts."

"The heck?" Shoving my hat back on my head, I get out of the Gator and stomp toward the house, heading straight for my office and powering up my computer.

"What are you going to do?" Nora is hot on my heels, dropping her weight in the seat opposite me as I angrily read over the email. Basically, Rod and Phil are calling us liars by claiming Big Bruiser was given to us in good faith and that we're expected to hold up our end of this imaginary deal. There's a line about not making contact with interested parties, but I'm far too incensed to adhere to any kind of rule since those rodeo folk are blatantly trying to swindle us.

"I'm gonna call Rod and tell him what I think about his claim."

Nora worries her lips together as I dial the rodeo's number and tap my fingers impatiently on my desk.

"Are you sure this is wise?" Her brows lift, eyes wide as she watches me with trepidation.

"Wise or not. There are things that need to be said." I nod at her fiercely before lowering the phone and putting it on speaker.

"Randy." Rod's voice sounds displeased the moment we connect. "I thought we were supposed to be communicatin' via our lawyers."

"This is ridiculous, Rod. You and I both know that bull was given to Josie and Sawyer as an engagement gift. Turnin' around and claimin' we owe you prized bull calves of your choosin' without any compensation is just plain stealin'. You set us up in an underhanded, cheatin' way and I ain't havin' it. The only way this is endin' is if you buy Bruiser back for the costs I've outlaid by takin' care of him thus far."

"You can't make me pay for a bull I already own!" Rod blurts.

"I can, and I will, because I'm the one who owns him as of right now. In the state of Alaska, hell, in the US of A, a gift, is a gift, is a gift. And if you take this to court, you're just gonna waste both of our time and money. Is this really how you wanna do business when we're all family now?"

I hear him suck in a deep breath before he finally exhales. "Look, I'm sorry this is puttin' a strain on things, Randy. But that bull is worth a heck of a lot more in stud fees than it is in the rodeo rink. So why on earth would I just hand him to y'all for free? That don't make a lick of sense to me."

Pursing my lips, I pinch the bridge of my nose, frustrated that this story is getting more and more twisted the more often it's told. "I don't pretend to understand what your thinkin' is,

Rod. But I do know how that bull came to be livin' here. If you want him back, you buy him back. Otherwise, as far as me and my ranch are concerned, this matter is closed."

With a huff of breath, I reach out and hang up the phone, ending the call before releasing a growl of displeasure.

"You think he'll back off?" Nora asks, not seeming fussed by my angry call.

Glancing up at her from where I'm now leaning on my desk, I slowly shake my head. "Not on your life. Seems to me they sent the bull to us after they were made to pull it from the ring when it attacked Sawyer. Then I reckon they got offers to use Bruiser as a stud and realized they let a pretty chunk of change slip through their fingers. Now, they're after us to make up for what they feel they lost."

"I'm so sorry you're having to deal with this." Nora stands and circles my desk, standing behind me and draping her arms over my shoulders. "I know you don't need the stress."

With a sigh, I lift a hand and wrap it around her forearm, leaning into her. "Stupid thing is, if they'd just asked for Bruiser back, I would've obliged. It's this whole 'you owe us' mentality that's got my hackles up. I don't operate like that—never have and never will—and I won't be forced into doin' something I'm not OK with just to please a grown man who's hell-bent on throwin' a tantrum to get his way."

"Is there anything I can do to help you feel better?" Nora whispers, her voice taking on a husky quality that instantly has my aggravation softening and my body stiffening in all the right ways as my attention shifts from my troubles to her.

"You could start by comin' even closer so I can show you just how much I appreciate all your help and support." Turning in my chair, I grab her hips and pull her up against me, allowing my hands to slide up the front of her thighs.

"Here's me wanting to show you how much I appreciate you," she whispers, glancing toward the closed office door as she carefully lowers to her knees in front of me, her fingers reaching for my belt as her mischievous eyes meet mine. "You think anyone will interrupt?"

"They're all busy doin' chores, darlin'," I murmur roughly, running my thumb along her jaw as looks up at me hungrily. "So 'no' is the only answer you need."

"In that case," she says, twisting my fly open. "All that's left for you to do is lean back and relax. It's time to let *me* take care of *you* for a change."

Letting out a low growl, I do exactly that, my fingers curling into her hair as she leans forward, pulling my dick from my jeans and wrapping those bright pink lips around my shaft, making all of my problems disappear with each delicious suck. If I wasn't in love before, I certainly am now. Because this woman is absolute perfection. The Mountain wouldn't have chosen her any other way.

## 25

## NORA

After a day full of client meetings at my Timber Falls office, I tie up a few loose ends in the office. Tapping out an email, I sing along to the radio, counting down the seconds to home time when I'm interrupted by my phone ringing with Mom's name flashing on the screen.

"Hey, Mom. Let me guess, you're checking to make sure I'm on my way home?"

"Hi. Well, yes, I was."

I frown when I pick up on a weird vibe in Mom's tone. "I'm about thirty minutes away from leaving. Why?"

"Good. That's good," she replies distractedly.

"Mom, what's *really* going on?" My Spidey senses are definitely pinging now.

"It's probably nothing. I was just wondering if you knew where Leah might be? She's not home from school yet, and I thought maybe she'd made arrangements with you and simply forgot to let *me* know. I know I shouldn't worry, but—"

"Old habits die hard, right?"

"Unfortunately, yes." Mom sighs. "I'm sure it's nothing. She's been doing so well lately and hasn't put a step wrong. But her phone just goes through the voicemail and I can't get a hold of her. Can you put an old woman's mind at ease and just check with that tracking app of yours?"

"Sure thing," I say, already putting her on speaker so I can do just that. A few moments later, I can see my daughter's location on the screen. Where I'd been expecting to find her hanging around the school, or maybe at Betty's Diner or even at Kinleyville Lake with some new friends, I get a surprise when I find her somewhere I never would've guessed–on the *ranch*. "What in the *world*?' I whisper.

"What? Please don't tell me she's back in Timber Falls or doing something crazy like going Anchorage again," Mom says, her voice resigned as she jumps to the worst-case scenario—understandable, given Leah's recent history...

"No, Mom. It's actually kind of good news... I think..."

"What does *that* mean?"

"She's at the ranch, Mom. No stress."

"There's no such thing as no stress with you *and* Leah in my life, Eleanor. *What* ranch?'

I snort because Mom's not exactly wrong. "Randy's ranch. Eagle Mountain."

"What? Oh gosh, did I forget she was working there today? I thought she doesn't work during the week?"

Mystery solved for the moment, at least. I breathe out a sigh of relief—albeit a slightly confused one. "You're right in that. She's not *supposed* to work during the week. That's time to get home and do her homework. And even if she wanted to go help out with the horses again, she should've asked us first. I'll head home now so I can stop by on my way home and bring her back with me."

"And maybe give her a little talk about not worrying her Nanny too," Mom says, her words laced with humor and relief.

"Yes, Mom. Can't have *dear old Nanny* thinking her daughter *and* granddaughter are running amok, right?"

"Hey! Enough with this old business. I'll have you know that I'm as fit as a fiddle and—"

I can't help but laugh. "As prickly as a Mama Bear missing her cubs?"

"Well, *that* I won't argue with," she says with a snort. "But don't be too hard on Leah. There are far worse places she could've been with far worse people. At least if she's hanging out at the ranch, she can't get into *too* much trouble."

"Yeah, I know. It's just a little frustrating, I guess. But I know if Randy had asked her to help out today, he'd have run it by me first, so I'm thinking this could just be Leah having a normal teenage moment of forgetfulness."

"Well, of course he would. Your Randy is responsible and thoughtful," she gushes, not even hiding her admiration for my man. If there was a Randy Barnes fan club, she'd be fighting me for its presidency. He's well and truly won my mother over without even trying. Then again, he already won *me* over a long time ago, so it's not that surprising, really. Even Leah has warmed up to him. Finding out that the mountain lore is in fact real and not just a whacked-out family legend or a fictional romance plot device has definitely helped. But also being given more jobs and responsibilities around the ranch has helped my daughter bloom. Things have been so great, even her attitude and demeanor have improved. She's *smiling* more, laughing more... and working at the ranch is no longer a dreaded event. Some mornings, she's even up and out of bed before the rest of us.

"Let me go find her and see what's going on. Randy has said reception can be spotty in some of the outlying fields, but I'll keep trying to call her, anyway. I'll be in touch when I find her."

"OK. And Eleanor?"

"Yeah, Mom?" I say as I shut down my computer and collect my purse and coat on my way out the door.

"Don't be too hard on my girl. Forgetting to tell us is a hell of a lot better than not telling us or lying. She's come so far. I don't want any of us to take two steps back. McIntyre women are going places in this town, remember?"

"We sure are," I say before saying goodbye and ending the call. After a quick goodbye to my assistant, I head for my car and bring up Leah's number, setting my cell in the cradle as I get myself strapped in and on the road. I've barely made it out of my parking spot when her voicemail kicks in before the call could even connect–she must be working toward the back of the property. And since she was chatting away excitedly about her weekend up at Horse Haven, my guess is she's snuck up there to spend more time with her new animal pals.

Well, I hope that's the reason, anyway. Because it's either the horses or the six foot two teenage ranch hand nephew of my boyfriend that's lured her up there. And as I drive my way from Timber Falls to Eagle Mountain, I really hope that it's the former. I'm too young to be a grandma.

~

AFTER LEAVING my car at Horse Haven and not seeing anyone around, I bring up my tracking app and let my phone lead the way, walking toward the fields in search of Leah. In my head, I'm hoping she isn't up to no good again, then tell myself off for instantly doubting my daughter when she's had such a huge change in behavior and attitude since moving to Kinleyville. Even her grades have gone up from low C's to B's across the board. I should be able to give her the benefit of the doubt by now, surely. But I think that there's always going to be that little voice at the back of my mind telling me to worry–whether she's sixteen or thirty-six.

Fifteen minutes of walking later, my sore feet are rueing the decision to trek through a ranch in formerly cute/now dust-covered suede kitten heels when I hear voices. Turning my head, I spot Leah, Sage, and Colton standing around a farm buggy of some sort with two of the wheels missing and the nose jacked up in the air. *Please don't tell me they've been joyriding...*

"Leah!" I call out as I get closer. She spins around and smiles, her eyes widening with surprise before a smile forms.

"Hey, Mom. What're you doing here? I thought you were back in Timber for work today?"

"Hey, Ms. McIntyre," Colton and Sage say in unison.

I narrow my eyes at them all before shooting Leah a questioning stare. To her credit, she holds her hands up in surrender. "I know. I didn't ask. But Sage asked if I wanted to come over after school and hang out, then we used the Gator to go check on the new orphaned foal Kendra rescued, but we didn't even get that far before we blew *two* tires, *and* blew a hose thing. So, of course, Colton had to come and rescue us."

Colton's lip twitches at Leah's clueless description. Sage just smiles at her friend.

"Leah, you know you need to tell us where you're going. Both your grandmother and I have been calling you and it's been going straight to voicemail."

Her brows furrow, genuine confusion with a tinge of guilt marring her expression. "I didn't reject your calls. My phone hasn't made a sound since we've been here." She reaches into the back pocket of her jeans, pulling out her handset and holding it up, her head dropping forward with a groan. "No service." She meets my eyes again. "I'm sorry. I honestly didn't think you'd mind me coming out here. We're weren't mucking around or getting into trouble. I swear, Mom. And I wasn't trying to be sneaky or disobey."

"It's true, Ms. McIntyre," Sage says, coming to Leah's defense. "We were only gonna be out here a couple of hours, but then the Gator broke down and Colton's been workin' fast as he can to get it working again."

Colton nods, apparently backing up his sister. "I thought I could at least get the Gator and the girls back to the barn, and if not, we were just gonna wait for Randy or some of the brothers to get back from replacing the boundary fence and then they could help us out." He glances Leah's way and I swear I spot a little tinge of pink in my daughter's cheeks. *Damn, Randy wasn't wrong about that.*

I switch my attention between all three teenagers. "You still should let us know where you're going, sweetheart. *Especially* if you're going somewhere with spotty reception. Nanny was worried and called me to track you. Thank god for satellites and tracking apps."

Leah's shoulders slump in relief as she rolls her eyes at the same time–a special talent only formerly surly teenagers possess, I've found. "So, am I in trouble, then?"

I shake my head and give her a soft smile, proud of her for so many things, but especially for owning up to today's misstep without any hesitation. I'm just about to say so when I hear the sound of an engine coming toward us. Turning toward the noise, I spot Randy speeding our way in a second Gator. He hops out and walks over to me, his features stressed and his body held tight.

"Hello, my love. I wasn't expectin' to see you 'til later," he says, not hiding his appreciation of my presence or my outfit from his gaze before he leans in and brushes his lips against mine.

"Yeah. Long story involving an impromptu after-school invite, spotty phone reception, the need for my daughter to have a homing beacon, and broken farm equipment."

Randy's expression turns confused before he looks at Colton. "You seen Cass around?"

Colton jerks his head from side to side. "Not for a few hours. Why's that?"

"Big Bruiser–the rodeo bull–is not where he should be, so I wanted to check and see whether Cass moved him and forgot to tell me."

"I don't remember seein' him move any of the animals around today," Colton adds.

"It's not like an animal *that* size is easy to lose. What if–" I stop myself mid-sentence, not wanting to verbalize my first instinct.

"What were you gonna say, darlin'?" Randy says, cupping his hand on my shoulder and giving it an encouraging squeeze. "What if...?"

"It's nothing. Just me thinking worst-case scenario."

Randy dips his head so his gaze is in line with mine. "Nora, tell me what you're thinking."

"OK. What if the rodeo took him back? Like re-possessing him."

"Shit," Colton mutters. "Didn't think of that."

Randy's eyes flash with shock, then narrow with anger. "Dammit. Those two-bit, cheatin', lyin', trickin' rodeo *clowns*." He starts pacing, spitting fire, and kicking the ground just like I imagine an angry, cornered bull would do. He jerks his gaze to Colton.

"You're in charge of the girls. Leave the Gator and walk back to the barn. Grab the horses and ride along the south boundary to tell everyone what's goin' on. Gather everyone outside the barn in thirty, so we can go on a search in case he just got loose." The young man lifts his chin, his shoulders squaring and his chest puffing out, and I can tell that he's taking the responsibility he's been given seriously. Which, I must say, makes me feel a hell of a lot better about him than I did ten minutes ago.

"Nora and I will head to the house. Looks like I've got another angry phone call to make to the damn rodeo," Randy explains through gritted teeth.

After that, there's nothing more to be said because Randy's tugging me toward the Gator and I'm left waving to the kids. It's then I remember that I was supposed to ring Mom back and update her. Just before Randy puts his foot down, I turn back to my daughter.

"Leah, Call Nanny as soon as you have reception and tell her we might be a little uh *late* for dinner."

"Got it," Leah says, immediately lifting her phone and walking around to try and get a few bars. "Oh wait! Can I ride a horse to help look too?"

"Sure!" I yell out, just as Randy turns on the engine and we're jetting away. There's only one thing on everyone's minds now–locate that damn bull.

## 26

## RANDY

"Thanks, chief," I say, my lips tight as I listen on the phone. "I'll be sure to let you know if we locate the animal ourselves."

"Nothing?" Nora asks when I replace the receiver in its cradle, placing my hands on my hips as I let out a long and heavy sigh. I've called every number I can think of for the rodeo and not one person has answered—not even when Josie and Sarah tried calling on my behalf. I figured that if they won't even speak to their own kin, then there definitely must be something amiss. I was left with no choice but to get the law involved so they can put out a BOLO or something so they can't get too far without being pulled over.

"Nope. But if it turns out they did take him, I swear to god it'll take a lot more than returnin' him and an apology to get me not to sue them all into poverty. I don't care if they're kin to Josie and Sarah. This kind of behavior just can't stand."

Nora comes up beside me and loops her arm through mine as she looks at me sympathetically. "I wish there was something more we could do," she says, sighing heavily. "You wanna get out there and help the others search? Might give you something to do besides wearing out the carpet with your pacing while waiting for the phone to ring?"

Pulling her into my arms, I hold her tight and breathe in her heady scent. It offers me calm and I lean down to press a kiss to the top of her head, taking a moment of quiet to just collect myself before I respond.

"Yeah," I say finally, as I let her go and grab my Stetson from off the desk. "Let's get in the truck and drive the perimeter to check in with everyone."

Grabbing a radio off the charging dock before we head outside to my truck, I open the passenger side door, waiting for Nora to get inside.

"Thanks for this," I say, leaning in and brushing my lips against hers as she pulls the belt across her lap. "Havin' you by my side in a crisis means a heck of a lot."

I don't think I've ever seen a bull move that fast before.

"Is that—"

"That's Bruiser," I say, slamming on my brakes and stopping the truck abruptly in the middle of the road. "He must have gotten out of his pen after all."

We watch in awe as all four come barreling toward us, bull in front, horses following up the rear. Bruiser's hooves pound into the ground so hard I'm surprised the earth isn't shaking at our feet. Dust swirls and storms in his wake, making it nearly impossible to see the riders on the horses at first glance. But we get a good glimpse after a while and realize very quickly these three kids are way in over their heads.

"Please tell me I'm not looking at my daughter riding full pelt on a horse while chasing an angry rodeo bull," Nora says as the group gets closer.

"I'm not a man who lies to the people he loves, Nora. So I don't think I can do that."

"Oh hell." Her hand goes to her mouth as she stares at the chaotic scene. Bruiser's eyes are wide with terror and his stride doesn't appear to be faltering whatsoever. If we stay parked across the road the way we are, he'll likely ram right into the side of us. And I don't need to go into detail about the kind of damage that force could do to the lot of us.

"Nora," I say quickly, unbuckling my seatbelt while throwing the truck into reverse and backing up slowly so as not to spook him into turning around. "I'll need you to drive this thing so I can get in the back and get a lasso ready."

"OK," she breathes, scrambling awkwardly across the seat to take the wheel while I swing out of the door to climb into the bed of the truck.

Nora steadies us out, keeping the speed just a little under the approaching animals while I ready my rope and position myself with one arm holding the roll bar and the other holding the lasso above my head.

"Hold the course, darlin'," I call out, my heart pounding in my chest because this could end terribly if I don't do it just right.

Bruiser releases an alarmed grunt, finally faltering when he gets a few yards from us. Nora slows a touch and I release the lasso, hooking Bruiser's right horn while Colton manages to lasso his snout. The bull rears back, but between the two of us, we get him under enough control that Nora gets the chance to radio for Cass and Jesse to bring the trailer to us. It's almost dark by the time we all make it back to the ranch house in one piece, and it's in that moment that I realize what an incredibly lucky man I am.

Not only do I have a family willing to drop everything to search for a pain-in-the-ass bull that I'm starting to think will forever be the bane of my existence, but I also have a beautiful woman by my side willing to do the same. And when we enter the ranch house to a fully set table and the scent of Ellie-Mae's cooking in the air, I know that I finally have everything I've ever wanted. And no fight with a rodeo over a bull is ever going to take that away from me.

"OK, you lot," Ellie-Mae calls out as we bustle inside the house. "How about you wash up, then come eat? I want to hear all about your search. I mean, where did Bruiser even go?"

That's when Leah and Sage look at each other and burst out laughing.

"What's so funny?" Nora asks, looking between them.

"Oh Mom," Leah says, unable to contain her cackling. "You don't wanna know what we saw."

"What do you mean?" I ask, turning my eyes on Colton, who's also trying not to laugh.

"Ah...Seems Bruiser has himself a girlfriend," he explains. "We found him romancin' a cow in the back paddock. And they...well... were havin' relations."

The entire house breaks into laughter—well, all except Cass. If this results in a pregnancy, it will definitely put a dent in his well-executed breeding plans...

## 27

## NORA

After we've all finished eating Ellie-Mae's delicious beef and mushroom casserole, we all sit back and let our stomachs settle. The teenagers huddle together, chatting and laughing, and much to my discomfort, there's no mistaking the low-key flirting and energy going on between Leah and Colton.

Randy loops his arm over the back of my chair and leans in to nuzzle my cheek. "Don't you worry about those two, darlin'. I'm keeping my eye on them, and Colton's given me his word that he won't go there. He may be a hormone-filled teenage boy, but he's not stupid enough to go against me."

I sigh. "Yeah, I get that. But having been a hormone-filled teenager, and now *having* one myself, I know what can happen when adults aren't around. Believe me..."

He presses his lips to the corner of my mouth. "I dunno. I think I might've liked hormone-filled Nora. Imagine the trouble you and I could've gotten up to," he says with a promising chuckle. *Great, now all I wanna do is recreate teenage trouble with him.*

"Well, now. Since Randy and Nora seem to be all lovey-dovey and totally wrapped up in each other, who do we think is gonna be next, y'all?" Ellie-Mae asks the table at large.

"Maybe we oughta be askin' Kendra that," Josie–Sawyer's fiancée–says. "She's the one with a direct line to the Mountain Spirit." All heads turn Kendra's way, Jesse chuckling as he sits back in his chair and shakes his head.

"Y'all know my wife doesn't tell us anything about what's comin' next. She doesn't even tell me and I'm the one who makes her–scrumppph." Kendra's hand darts out to cover her husband's mouth, her eyes narrowing at him.

"Don't you dare speak about your wife like that at the dinner table," she teases, pulling her hand away from an amused Jesse who's quick to drop a kiss on the end of her nose.

Sawyer chuckles, then looks around the table with a keen eye. "Since there are only three single Barnes men left, I'm thinkin' we should take bets," he says, rubbing his hands together.

Fixing his eyes on Cass, he stops and nods thoughtfully. "What about you, young Caspian? You feelin' ready to hear the Mountain's Call?"

Cass almost chokes on thin air, his face going bright red as he shakes his head emphatically.

"Cass is married to his work. Aren't ya, brother?" Jasper pipes up, reaching over and patting his brother on the back.

"I'm also not *young*," he retorts as he catches his breath. "I'm thirty-one and you're talkin' about me like I'm a dreamy-eyed kid."

"Practically ancient then," Colton teases, earning himself a giggle from Leah.

My mouth falls open as I make eye contact with my daughter. "I'll have you know that thirty-one is *not* old, thank you very much." I turn to Randy and settle into his side with a pout. "Besides, you're only as old as you feel."

Leah responds with another giggle, undoubtedly biting her tongue over a retort involving the time when she busted Randy and me, making out like teenagers at the lookout a while back.

While the others return to their own conversations, Randy turns his mouth to my ear. "You feel pretty damn good if my memory serves me correctly," he whispers, making me tremble and leaving me wondering whether it's too late to plan a sleepover.

The screech of a chair leg against the floor steals me from my dirty thoughts, though, as Cass stands from the table. "Randy, I'm just gonna go through the logs in your office and check the effect of this *unfortunate* coupling. Yeah?"

"Sure thing. It's in the folder on top of my desk, right where you left it," my man replies.

Cass nods. "I'll be back." He disappears down the hall toward Randy's office, and the after-dinner conversation continues. But not without interruption...

Moments later, there's the unmistakable sound of tires coming to a stop outside the house. Randy straightens, lifting a brow and switching his gaze between the Barnes men at the table before he presses a quick kiss to my temple and moves to his feet. He swings open the door to be met by two police officers–a man and a beautiful blonde female who looks like she could be a model if she ever wanted a career change. Her piercing gray eyes are soft and gentle, yet also guarded. Soft and hard at the same time.

"Officers?" Randy says.

The male officer looks into the room, nodding to all of us before turning his gaze back to Randy. "Good evening, all. Sorry to disrupt your evening. But the chief wanted us to follow up on your call from earlier."

Randy steps back and sweeps his arm out. "I understand. Do you want to come in?" The officers remove their hats and move just inside the kitchen, Ellie-Mae rising to her feet and moving toward them.

"Howdy. Do y'all want some coffee? It's no hassle to rustle some up for y'all."

The man smiles. "Thanks for the offer, Ellie-Mae, but we don't need to stay long. Officer Jones and I just need to check that everything is in hand and that the complaint can now be marked as resolved." His lips quirk up into a grin. "You know how it is. Dotting the i's and crossing the t's."

"Sure thing, Officer Landry. Let's call it a rain check then. We're all about supporting the town's hard-working law enforcement," Ellie says with her typical, affable charm.

"Appreciate the hospitality. But we won't keep you long." Officer Landry turns to Randy. "Chief Tucker says you located the missing bull."

"Yep. It appeared he escaped his lodgings in search of greener pastures." Muted snickers and chuckles fill the air, Randy's lips twitching too. The officers grin at each other.

"I see. So no crime committed then after all," Landry muses.

"Might have to ask his female bovine acquaintance about that," Jesse mutters, earning more laughter.

Both Officer Jones and Landry's brows lift at that. "OK then. I guess this case is officially closed."

"It appears so. Please pass on my apologies to the Chief for wasting his valuable time."

"No harm, no foul, Randy. You know we're always here to help when needed."

"Just not when it's an over-amorous bull, right, officer?" Ellie-Mae chimes.

Landry just nods.

"And you've contacted the rodeo about this? We spoke to a Mr. Rod Moore, and he assured us that he was a thousand miles away and had no involvement in the bull's disappearance."

Randy grimaces and rubs the back of his neck. "That's gonna be the awkward call I've got to look forward to."

Landry nods sympathetically. "I bet."

It's then that Cass walks back into the room. "Hey, Randy, I've just been checking our breeding log in your office and if Bruiser managed to inseminate that co–" He abruptly stops talking at the same time he trips over his feet, righting himself while staring dumbfounded at the cops–in particular, the beautiful blonde. *What in the world?*

"Amanda?" he chokes out, half shocked-half awed.

"Caspian?" she mouths, her eyes widening before they warm, a wide blinding smile transforming her face. "I didn't expect to run into you. I thought you'd have been long gone, saving animals from extinction or something."

Sawyer walks up to his cousin and wraps his arm around his shoulders. "Nah. Cass got his degree then decided savin' animals right here at the ranch was where his heart was. Right, buddy?" He sweeps his gaze toward the rest of the family. "Amanda here was Prom Queen, Class President, and Miss Kinleyville for two years in a row when Jasper, Cass, Finn, and Remy were all at school. Then she left us all for the big city lights."

Cass's cheeks turn a tinge of pink and it's obvious he doesn't like being the center of attention. Even still, he can't seem to tear his eyes off Amanda. "I didn't know you were back."

"Oh, those big city lights were a little *too* bright for me. Seems home is still Kinleyville for me too," she says cheerfully, but there's something behind her words that has those ever-trusty Spidey senses of mine not just tingly, they're vibrating because it's obvious that something did or should have happened between Cass and Amanda in the past.

*Now I really wanna know what's going on here.*

My romance-loving heart is swooning at all the possibilities. Is it a second chance love story waiting to be told? Unrequited love? Maybe a beauty and the quiet, unassuming geek situation? And we all know what happens to those quiet, unassuming geeks from school...

Kendra catches my eye and winks across the table at me, her gaze twinkling with amusement like she knows exactly what's running through my head. "Guess who's next," she mouths before shifting her attention back to watch Cass and the mysterious female cop.

Cass and Sawyer continue chatting with the two police officers for a moment longer, Randy joining their little huddle in the kitchen.

Then a while later, when the police bid their farewells and Randy shuts the door behind them, his eyes meet mine, and I can't help but smile over at him, earning a bemused and somewhat confused grin in return. Because if the ranch's seer is telling me that Cass and the mysterious Amanda are next, that must mean that our Call–mine and Randy's–is complete.

Which also means that all that's left for us is the best part of any love story–the happily ever after.

And I, for one, can't *wait* for that.

## 28

# RANDY

"My accusation was unfounded, and as a show of my regret and in the spirit of puttin' this all behind us, I'd like to offer you a deal," I say into the phone as Cass, Jesse, Jasper, Josie and Sarah listen in patiently while I talk to Rod about Bruiser. While I feel somewhat bad for jumping to conclusions when he went missing, I'm still not willing to hand all of our bull calves sired by Bruiser over to the rodeo free of charge. But I am willing to offer them a maximum of two bull calves each breeding season at cost. If we can agree to that, we can put this entire drama to bed and skip the thousands of dollars in lawyers' fees by keeping this out of the courts.

Rod mulls over my offer, muffling the phone while he discusses it with his brother. I can hear their back and forth, so I already know what he's going to say when he pulls his hand away from the receiver again.

"That seems more than fair," Rod agrees after several minutes. "You'll be sure to let us know as soon as the calves are born?"

"Of course," I agree, breathing easier now that things seem to be wrapping up nicely.

"OK then," he says, asking for the phone to be handed to his daughter before we say a quick goodbye.

Cass, Jesse, Jasper, and I leave Josie and Sarah in the office to have a private chat with their fathers, heading into the living room where the others are all waiting to hear the news.

I drop my weight onto the sofa next to Nora and sigh. "Well?" she asks, turning her knees toward me. "What'd they say?"

Lifting my head, I meet her eyes before looking around the room at the sea of expectant faces. It's getting late, and normally the family would have dispersed to their own cabins by now or we would've retired to the fire pit to share a drink and chat. Tonight, though, we've all stayed in the ranch house hoping the saga of Bruiser the Bull could be sorted finally.

Resting my hand on Nora's knee, I allow a smile to take over my face. "They accepted," I announce, earning myself a loud whoop from the entirety of the Barnes family.

"This calls for a celebration if ever I heard a need for one!" Ellie-Mae calls out, hugging her husband, Miller, and kissing him hard on the mouth. "I'm so damn relieved."

"Me too," he says, turning to face me. "Want me to call Micah and let him know it's settled?" Micah is Miller's homestead kin from where he grew up on Bear Mountain. He's a lawyer and always more than happy to lend a legal hand when needed.

"That'd be great, Miller. Thanks. Tell him I'll call him in the next day or two to tie up any loose ends, too."

"Will do, boss," he says with a smile and a salute as comments of relief continue to be made all round.

"I think this calls for a grown-up sleepover too," Nora says, snuggling into my side while everyone's attention shifts to the beers Ellie and Miller are now handing out.

"I love the way your mind works, darlin'," I say, leaning in to nuzzle my nose against hers. "I can't think of anyone else I wanna celebrate with."

Her voice is breathy when she replies. "I'll get Leah home once the excitement dies down and then come back when she's gone to bed."

"OK. I'm thinkin' of suggestin' a time when you won't have to leave though," I say, lifting my brow slightly as she tilts her head in question.

"What do you mean?"

"Well, things are gettin' pretty serious between us now, and Leah seems real happy here..."

"Yes..."

"And I thought that maybe you, me, and her might be gettin' ready to transition to a life together. It doesn't have to be right away. We can start slow—maybe weekends on the ranch, a day or two during the week. Until it just makes sense for you to be here all the time."

"Are you asking me to move in with you, Randy Barnes?" she asks, looking up at me with a slow-growing grin on her face.

I run my thumb down the side of her face, pausing at her chin before I take her mouth in mine. "Yeah, darlin'. I want you with me always."

"I want that too," she whispers, snuggling in a little closer. "And I really love it here, Randy. Leah does as well, so I don't think she'll fight me on it. I do have to think about Mom, though."

"I understand, Nora. I'm sure she'll be happy for you," I say, hoping that's true.

"I'm absolutely sure that she will be. But I need to talk to her. I want to make sure she doesn't feel like we're abandoning her."

"Well, if she's feeling a little funny about the change, she's more than welcome to join us here, too. We've got a stack of space on the ranch. Between us, we've built a bunch of cabins and we'll be more than happy to put one up for her too. Whatever she wants. I know y'all come as a package deal. The last thing I ever wanna do is pull apart the McIntyre girls. "

"Oh, Randy," she says, her eyes brimming with emotion. "You just amaze me with your generosity."

"I only want to make sure you, me, and Leah are happy...together as a family. Your mom too."

Placing my hand in hers, I draw her in for another kiss. I plan to change Nora McIntyre's name to Mrs. Barnes as soon as possible, so the sooner our living situation is sorted out, the better. I'll do whatever it takes to make Nora and everyone she cares about feel happy and well looked after. I've been doing it for years with my own relatives, putting their needs ahead of mine. But now, it's time to think about what I want. And that's Nora. I know in my heart that our Call is almost complete.

## 29

## NORA

We've been in Kinleyville for four months now, and the whole working from home plan continues to go well. I haven't lost any clients because of the move either. In fact, the business continues to go from strength to strength, with Randy recommending my wealth management services to the founding brothers at Bear Mountain Homestead and even Aster Hollingsworth herself. Now I have clients in Kinleyville, and the other mountain towns of Woodward Valley and Kenshaw–all towns living in the shadow of mystical mountains with their own generous matchmaking spirits.

Diana is still my assistant, and we still have access to our office in Timber Falls, but we now share it with the law firm from next door since we only visit once every few weeks for client meetings. This means I'm home most of the time and get to spend it with Mom and Leah–as well as visiting the ranch more often. Because when Randy sets his mind on something, he's proven himself to be more determined than I ever gave him credit for. When he said he wanted to work toward a life where all of us would live at Eagle Mountain with him, he meant it. Now we're almost there as much as we're here at home.

It hasn't just been good for me though, it's also meant Sage and Leah have been able to become the best of friends. On the nights we stay out there, the girls go to and from school together, and they also volunteer at Horse Haven a few afternoons a week and every Saturday. They love helping Kendra, Molly, and Josie with horse therapy courses for disabled and disadvantaged children. Seeing the change in Leah has made me the proudest mom in the whole of Kinleyville. She's found her passion and I'll forever be grateful to Randy and the day he suggested my daughter should work on the ranch. It was definitely the catalyst that led to this amazing change and growth in her—and for me. Moving towns for a fresh start has turned out to be the best thing we've ever done.

"Hey Mom," I say as I walk through the front door on a Friday afternoon after another day trip to Timber Falls. "What's going on?"

"Oh good, you're home. I need you to call Randy and ask him to come for dinner," she says, bustling about like a headless chicken, obviously flustered as she sets the table. What I don't know is why...

"OK... is this just an impromptu thing or has something happened?"

"I may have done something a little wild today, and now I'm a bit lost as to what to do about it," she rushes out, stopping what she's doing and staring at me.

Not once in all of my years have I seen my mother this... nervous... I cross the room and drop my purse and computer bag on the kitchen counter before crossing to the refrigerator, grabbing two glasses and a bottle of wine before urging my mother to join me. She huffs out a breath and takes a stool opposite me. I wait until she's had her first sip before pressing further.

"Mom, what's going on? You're as nervous as a long-tailed cat in a room full of rocking chairs. What on earth could you have done to have you so on edge?"

Her cheeks flush pink as her fingers toy with the stem of crystal. "I was in town today and Stanley Morrison from the Boat Shop asked if I'd like to go to dinner with him, and instead of accepting, I invited him over to a family dinner with all of us here."

Understanding dawns. "Neutral ground, good call, Mom. I'm happy for you. That's awesome news. I know you two have been chatting at the Town Hall Bingo nights."

Mom's shoulders relax, and I realize that her nerves must've been about telling me. Which is ridiculous, because I've only ever wanted my mom to be happy, just like that's all she's ever wanted for me.

I take on a motherly tone, reaching out and covering her hand with mine. "Now, Mom. You putting your life on hold and dedicating everything to this family has taught your daughter and granddaughter one thing–that we're loved," I say, repeating the same thing she said to me before we moved towns. "And I know Leah and I have been spending a lot of time at the ranch lately, so–"

Mom's eyes widen, and she shakes her head from side to side. "No, Eleanor. Don't you worry about me. My girls are moving on and toward a big and bright future. One has found the love of her life and the other is making new friends and discovering a whole new world out there." She takes a deep breath and sends me a gentle, loving smile. "I told you before we moved here that I wanted you to start living your life, and you're doing that. I'm so proud of the woman you've become, Eleanor. Leah is on the right track now and doing so well in school. And I've never seen her smile as much as I have done lately. All I've ever wanted for both of my girls is to see you both happy. And watching you fall head over heels for a good man like Randy Barnes has shown me that he was the missing piece you needed. I'm genuinely over the moon for you, dear."

I tilt my head and study her. "And is Stanley that missing piece for *you*?"

She winks at me. "Oh, I don't know about that. But I think it's worth dipping my toes in the water, so to speak."

"Are you sure you're OK, though?"

"Eleanor, don't you be worrying about me. I'm happy. I'm just a bit nervous now that this dinner is actually happening. It's been well over thirty years since I've cooked dinner for a man."

I roll my eyes. 'Mom, you cooked Randy dinner here just last week."

She waves her hand in the air and blows her lips, making a pfft sound. "Randy doesn't count. He's nearly my son. He's family." God, that feels good to hear.

I smile at her. "I love that you feel that way."

"Well, of course I do. If you don't think that man is head over heels for you and for Leah, then I haven't done my job raising you right. You're that man's sun, his whole world now revolves around my two girls. That's the kind of man a mother wants for her daughter."

"I actually think that means you have done your job right, Mom."

"Well, I think that deserves a toast before I have another little breakdown over making a pot roast for the first man to make my heart skip a beat in a long, long time–and it not being tachycardia," she says with a smirk and a little giggle as she raises her glass in the air and clinks it with mine. I snicker along with her because I've never seen Mom like this. She's so damn cute when she's crushing on a man. And after seeing Stanley in town a few times, I can't blame her for getting flustered. He might be getting on in years, but he's certainly easy on the eyes. I imagine he was incredibly handsome in his youth. Mom has a good eye.

"Right. Well, we need a plan of attack, and we need reinforcements. Randy was going to drop Leah off after she'd finished at Horse Haven, so I'll just give him a call and invite him in for dinner too. Maybe we'll just stay here tonight since we were spending the weekend at the ranch, anyway."

Mom nods, agreeing with my plan. I press on. "And while I'm doing that, you can check on the roast–because I know you'll worry about it anyway–and then you're going to finish that wine and go have a shower and pretty yourself up for your date." I narrow my eyes at her. "And learn from my mistakes, mother. Dress to impress, not for a business meeting, yeah?"

She giggles and shakes her head. "I'm being silly, I know it. I'm far too old to date. Aren't I?" There's a sliver of vulnerability and uncertainty in her tone that warms my heart.

"Mom, you are *never* too old to be happy. You deserve just as much happiness–if not more–than everyone else in this family. I can see how much you like Stanley, and I love that you're embarking on this whole new adventure. You always said the McIntyre women were going places in this town, and now look at us."

"I love you, Eleanor. You're the best thing that ever happened to me. You and Leah. And I can't wait to see where life is going to take all of us."

"Me too, Mom. Me too," I say, walking around the island and pulling her in for a big hug.

When I step back, though, I pin her with a stare. "Now, we have a plan. I call, you check, then I finish cleaning up while you get ready for your date. You with me?" I say, sounding more like a motivational life coach than I ever thought I would.

"Yes, ma'am. Gosh, who'd have thought I raised such a bossy daughter," she mutters, leaving me to giggle to myself as she goes to check on the dinner and I pull my phone out of my purse to call Randy.

Life is good. Honestly, it's so good, I can't imagine it getting any better. Then again, I'm in love with my soulmate, and as long as I'm by his side, I know life will be nothing short of perfect.

Because neither one of us would want it any other way.

## 30

# RANDY

"Is this going to take much longer?" Leah gripes, pushing a snow-heavy branch out of the way as we trek toward the greatest place on the ranch. "The ground is mush. Not sure why you think the day after an early snowfall is the perfect time for a picnic."

I shoot a smile over my shoulder as Leah looks at me in that way teenagers do—like I have no idea what I'm doing, and they're the only ones with all the answers. "We're almost there," I say. "I'm sure you can make it." In answer, she blows a raspberry between her lips at me.

"Cheer up, sweetheart," Beverly says, a slight puff in her voice as she soldiers on without complaint. "If your old nanny can make this walk, then I think those young legs of yours will be right in their element. Isn't it just beautiful out here? I've always loved the smell of the earth after the first snow of the season. There's still a warmth underfoot, and the cold seems to release a crisp earthy scent that's even sweeter than summer rain."

"All I smell is mud," Leah responds, although there's less grouch in her tone now as she tries to catch the scent her grandmother is talking about. "And...pine, I think."

"I smell possibility," Nora says after a deep inhale. She walks alongside me, a blanket draped over her arm as I carry the picnic basket filled with a great assortment of food. Ellie-Mae is the one who put it together for me, which is something I'm sure we'll all be grateful for since my various attempts at cooking have all ended with a meal tasting of charcoal or an inedible disaster resulting in a last-minute pizza order from town. But since today is a special day, I wasn't leaving anything to chance. Even if that meant asking Ellie-Mae for help.

"Possibility has a smell?" Leah laughs. "Maybe it's a good thing you're an accountant, Mom. Wordsmithing really isn't your thing."

"Is that how you talk to your mother on her birthday?" I tease, shooting her a look that makes her smile back, an understanding twinkle in her eye.

"She knows I'm just kidding," she says, shooting me a smirk before adding, "Or am I?"

Nora laughs after catching the exchange between her daughter and me. "It's OK, you two. I know I'm not gifted in words. Numbers are my jam. But it doesn't change the fact that the air just feels...different up here."

"You know what?" Leah says, stopping suddenly and holding her hand up like she can feel it on the tips of her fingers. "I actually think you're right about that. It feels..." She furrows her brow, wiggling her fingers as she searches, "almost warm."

"Magic," Beverly says, her hand to her chest as she stares up at the powder-dusted boughs. "This place has always felt like magic...even before we knew it was its own brand of special."

It's those words that cause me to break into a smile before I start toward the tree line, pulling bushes aside like a curtain leading into another world.

"What is this place?" Nora asks, looking around in awe as we move from the cold into the almost tropical warmth of Paradise Springs.

Setting the picnic gear aside, I slide my arm around the waist of the woman I love, tugging Nora toward me before I gesture to the bubbling water. "This is my family's sacred spring. There's one on each of the mountains, and it's where the spirit is felt the strongest. We come here for contemplation, for completion, and sometimes, just for a swim in the warm water."

Leah gasps, pulling her warm jacket from her shoulders and dumping it on the ground while simultaneously shucking her boots. "Now I know why you said to bring our swimming stuff," she says, wonder in her voice and expression as she moves to the water's edge and dips her toe in. "It's so warm! Like a little pocket of paradise."

"Bet you don't think this picnic is such a dumb idea after all, huh?" Beverly calls out, chuckling as she sets out the blanket on the soft grass.

Nora and I move to help her, and by the time we're all sitting down, Leah is already stripped down to her swimwear, sinking into the warmth of the spring. "This place is amazing!" she yells with childlike wonder, making me grin. *She's definitely come a long way from our first awkward meeting.*

"Sometimes you forget how young she really is," Beverly says, a soft smile on her face as she watches her granddaughter frolicking about in the water.

"Oh, she'll always be a little girl to me," Nora says, resting her head on my shoulder as I pour hot coffee from a Thermos into three mugs and hand them around. "I think that's why I fought so hard to keep her young. I wasn't ready for her to grow up." She sniffles. "I don't think I ever will be, if I'm being honest."

"That's something I've always loved about this ranch," I say, hugging her to me as I sip at the brew. "It gives kids the space they need to grow, along with the freedom to play. Hell, me and my brothers still get into the rough housin' whenever the mood suits."

"It really is a dream here, Randy," Beverly says. "And I'm really grateful to you that you're sharing it with us all."

"You know, I've been talkin' a lot to Nora and Leah about makin' their move out to the ranch a more permanent thing," I say, meeting Beverly's eyes. "And I was kind of hopin' you might like to place here too. The ranch house is plenty big enough for all of us without trippin' over each other. Or, if you'd rather, we can put a cabin up for you close by. You'll have privacy and still have total access to your girls. The last thing I'd ever wish to do is split up the McIntyre women of Kinleyville."

Beverly reaches out and places a gentle hand on my upper arm, smiling. "That's incredibly kind of you, Randy. And I know that your heart is in the right place. Nora and Leah have been the center of my world for so long that it's a big change for us to be apart. But truthfully, I welcome the change. And despite your very kind offer, I think I'd like to stay in the house in Kinleyville for the moment—if that's OK with Beau and Molly, of course. It allows me to walk into town, and I've made quite a few new friends there. So I want the chance to spread my wings and explore a little too. I hope I'm not hurting anyone's feelings."

"Oh, Mom," Nora says, handing me her mug as she shifts toward her mother and hugs her tight. "You aren't hurting anything. We just want you to be happy and to feel like you have a place with us no matter where we are in this world."

"That's right," I add. "You're family to all of us Barnes-folk now, Beverly. So, whatever you decide will be just fine with us. As long as we get to see plenty of you 'round the dinner table, of course. And the offer is always open. Whenever you feel you're ready to join us here on the ranch, you'll always be welcomed with open arms."

"Now that I've tried Ellie-Mae's cooking?" Beverly says with a raised brow. "You couldn't keep me away if you tried."

"Why are we keeping Nanny away?" Leah asks, pushing water from her face as she walks toward us, taking the towel her mother offers her before she sits down.

"We're not keeping her anywhere," Nora says with a laugh. "We were just discussing our moving plans. Nanny wants to stay on in the house so she can keep seeing her new friends."

"New boyfriend, more like," Leah says, waggling her brows as she pulls a lemon bar from inside the picnic hamper. "And y'all were worried about me and boys. Look at you two—all loved up and cozy while I do the hard work of rehabilitating horses and gettin' good grades at school. My, how the tables seem to have turned." She clicks her tongue, making me chuckle.

"She's not wrong." Nora laughs as she places her arm around her daughter and hugs her tight. "You know I'm obscenely proud of all you've achieved this year, right?"

Leah smirks and pulls away slightly. "Yeah, Mom. I know. You don't need to go all mushy on me. Save it for boyfriend."

Laughter reigns free as Nora releases her girl, but all I manage is a nervous grin because it's in that moment I see an opening to bring up the very important reason for bringing them all the way up here. "Speaking of bein' a boyfriend," I start, leaning to the side and reaching into my pocket as all eyes land on me. "I'm hopin' that'll change when I show y'all, well, this."

My fingers clasp around the ring box I placed in my pocket before we set out this morning, pulling it out and holding the dark velvet box for all to see.

"Oh my god," Leah gasps, her eyes going wide as she looks from her mother to me. "Mom! Is that what I think it is?"

"Randy?" Nora's eyes go wide, completely focused on the box. "Is that what we think it is?"

My heart sticks in my throat as I shift my weight to one knee and open the box. So many things could go wrong in this moment. I took a risk doing this with us all together like this today, but for some reason, nothing feels more right because it means Leah and Beverly are included in everything from now on—as family.

"Do you see this, Nanny?" Leah squeals, practically bouncing with excitement.

"I do. And I hope it's going to end exactly the way I think it is," Beverly whispers, the hope in her voice unmissable.

"With a happily ever after?" I ask, quirking my brow as my eyes stay locked with my girl's.

"That depends," Nora starts, a sly smile curving her mouth. "Are you gonna ask me? Or are you just gonna kneel there and show me?"

I scooch a little closer, grinning even harder. "Can't I do both?" I say, pulling the ring from the box and taking her hand in mine.

"Nora McIntyre. I've admired you from afar since the moment you blew into town stampin' your foot and tellin' me how money works and proclaimin' I had rocks in my head whenever I tried to tell you otherwise. You're smart, you're gorgeous, and if it wasn't for you, holdin' my hand and guidin' me this entire way, the ranch —and my life—wouldn't be as amazin' as it is today. You complete me in ways I can't even begin to understand. You've given me love, you've given me family"—I lift my gaze and smile at both Leah and Beverly—"and if you're all willin' to have me, I like to make this feelin' here official and make you mine forever. Will you marry me, Nora?"

Her eyes fill with tears as her hand goes to my cheek, the ring still resting between my fingers. "Randy Barnes, you make me feel like the most important piece of your beautiful mountain-living puzzle, and I love you so much for it. If you asked me to fly to the moon on Big Bruiser's back—I'd do it, because as crazy as anything may seem, you make everything seem possible. So when you ask me to marry you, there's no question. You bring only good into my life, and I can't wait to give all that good back to you."

"Is that a yes?" I ask, taking her hand in mine and holding the ring just above her nail.

She nods adamantly. "It's a yes, Randy. A big, fat, emphatic yes! Now put the damn ring on me so we can get on with this picnic. I'm starved!" she adds with a laugh as Leah cheers at her mother's words.

"It's a yes. She said yes!" Nora's mom laughs, clapping loudly, then wiping away happy tears too. "I couldn't have wished for a better man to take care of my girls."

"Why, thank you, Beverly," I say, turning my eyes her way as she gives me a teary nod.

"And I couldn't ask for a better guy to be my stepdad," Leah says. "I'm so happy for you both, but I'm gonna be a little selfish here and say I'm real happy for me, too. I love this place, and I honestly couldn't see myself living anywhere else in this world."

Nora's eyes flit to mine as she lifts her brows and leans in close. "Sounds like that Mountain Spirit of yours has been collecting new recruits," she says.

Chuckling, I pull her in close. "Ours, darlin'. The Call happened to both of us. So the spirit cares about us both, as well as everyone we're connected to."

"I'm really starting to like that idea," she says, resting her hands against my chest. "Almost as much as I like you."

"Like?" I jerk my head back and she laughs, rolling her eyes.

"OK. *Love*."

"That's better," I say, lowering my face until my lips touch hers. Then I seal our proposal with a breath-stealing kiss, knowing in my heart that the Call is complete, and that this is just the beginning of our happiness. The hard part is behind us. We're a family now. A happy one at that, and as long as we love each other every day as hard as we do today, we'll always be this damn happy.

## 31

## NORA

"Yes, Randy. Please... Please..." I beg as my fiancé buries himself in me from behind. I'm on my hands and knees, Randy standing beside the bed, his hips pistoning back and forth, his grunts and my muffled moans filling the air as we soar higher and higher.

"Come for me, darlin'. Wanna feel you cling to me," he growls, speeding up his thrusts as my vision goes white and pleasure so good and right and mind-blowing courses through me, wave after wave of euphoric, orgasmic bliss that has my body collapsing into the bed just as Randy groans a low guttural "Nora," and succumbs to his own satisfying conclusion.

"Fuck, Nora. Every time with you just keeps getting better and better," he murmurs as he drapes his body over my back and nuzzles at my neck. I reach back and glide my fingers into his head, loving the feel of his weight against me. His warmth, his strength, all of it reminds me that this wonderful man is pledging his troth to me–and I can't even remember if we ever did get to date number five. All I know is I didn't need five dates to know Randy Barnes was the one and only man for me. I think I knew that the first time I met him.

He goes to roll off me, but I flex my fingers and mutter my discontent. I'd stay with him like this forever if I could, but unfortunately, work and duty calls.

Randy chuckles before bracing himself on one arm and turning my face toward his, kissing me soft and slow, then deeper, longer, until I'm moaning and squirming beneath him again. He pulls back and smiles down at me, his dark eyes shining. "We'll continue this tonight, darlin'. But we need to get up and start our day."

I roll over, loving the way Randy's eyes darken as they roam over my naked form. "I thought we just *started* our day in our own unique, *very* enjoyable way." I shoot him a devilish grin.

"You're gonna be the death of me, Nora McIntyre."

"Soon to be Nora Barnes," I add.

He gets to his feet before bending down and hooking his arms under me, lifting my body and cradling me to him as he turns and walks toward his bathroom. "Shower."

I tilt my head and meet his eyes. "Shower sex?"

He groans and nips at my bottom lip. "Death of me, darlin'," he mutters with a smile.

I grip his hair and hold his mouth to mine. "But what a way to go, old man."

∽

Randy, Cass, and I huddle together against the cold of the changing season as we stand outside the paddock where all the pregnant heifers are grazing. They'll carry all through the winter, and when Spring comes, they'll be all giving birth to a bunch of new little calves, further increasing the stock numbers here at Eagle Mountain ranch.

"They're looking good," Cass says, gazing out over the herd. "And they're all healthy and doing well. Even after losing a bull calf or two to the rodeo, this is gonna be our best breeding season yet."

Randy claps him on the back. "And it's all thanks to you. Your knowledge and hard work continues to benefit all of us, Cass. I hope you know just how much we all appreciate it."

Cass grins at his cousin. "It's not work when you love what you do. Numbers-whiz Nora here can attest to that, I bet," he says, nodding my way.

"I just crunch the figures and approve the spending. Nothing like helping create new life and looking after the land like you all do."

Randy wraps his arm around my waist and pulls me in close. "We all play our part. Every little thing we do helps contribute to the ranch as a whole."

"Sure does. The Mountain Spirit must be feeling particularly bountiful this year though. We've never had fertility rates this high."

"Must be something in the water," I mutter under my breath.

Randy quirks a brow as he looks down at me. "Why's that?"

"Um..." I bite my lip, tossing up whether now is the best time.

Because this morning while Randy was in the kitchen making us coffee, I decided to take a test, part hopeful, part excited that maybe Randy and I had—albeit a little sooner than planned—created a new life together. We've talked about what we want in our future and both of us were on board with increasing our family. I even talked with Leah and made sure she was OK with us giving her a little brother or sister one day, and I don't think I've ever seen my daughter more excited about anything in her entire life.

So as I waited impatiently in our bathroom, my eyes glued to that pregnancy test, my nerves shot, my excitement tempered to not get ahead of myself, I closed my eyes and offered up a silent request to the Montain Spirit to give Randy one more reward for his lifetime of service to the ranch. I've known him long enough to know that he has never once complained about putting his life on hold for the good of his family. He also never complained when all of his brothers and a cousin or two heard the Call before him. So now that it's *his* turn, I want everything for him and more. It's the least he deserves.

When those two little lines finally appeared, I burst into tears. And ever since then, I've been trying to work out the best moment to tell my soon-to-be husband the news.

Cass eyes me suspiciously before a slow-growing smile curves his lips.

"I think that's my cue to leave." He steps forward and hugs me. "Congratulations, Nora. You're about to make my cousin the happiest man on Eagle Mountain." Then he moves away and climbs atop his horse, Randy watching him with a puzzled gaze.

"You do know you're next, right?" I call out just as he positions himself in the saddle.

"For what?" Cass asks, brows furrowed.

"Your time is coming, Cass. You're going to be rewarded just like we have."

Randy chuckles. "Reckon she's talkin' about your beauty queen turned cop, cousin."

Cass cocks his head. "You a fortune teller now, Nora?"

I grin over at him. "Nope. I was just in that room with you and Officer Jones. A woman knows these things. I think you should keep your eyes open and prepare your heart for one hell of a ride. It's never too late to rediscover love, you know…"

Cass tips his hat wordlessly before he digs his heels into the sides of his stallion, turning his head and leaving us alone in the middle of God's country, in my new home, the Mountain standing majestic and statuesque behind us.

Turning to Randy, I find his warm gentle eyes studying me as he reaches for my hips and pulls me into him. "You were saying?" he murmurs.

"It's never too late to rediscover love?"

"Before that…"

"Um…"

"About something being in the water…"

"Um…"

"Nora, darlin'," he says, smoothing his hands around to rest over my stomach, making my breath catch and my heart jump. "You carryin' my baby?"

I nod, tears welling at the absolute joy written all over my man's face, his own eyes glistening with emotion as he lowers his face to mine until he's all I can see. "You were already my blessing and my reward, Nora McIntyre. But now you've just become my miracle. God damn, I love you."

"I love you too," I choke out just before Randy wraps me up and slams his mouth down on mine, kissing me boneless and, as always, holding me up as he does it.

It's then that I soak it all in and realize that my soulmate is right. I'm his miracle, but he is also mine.

And with the proof of our love growing inside of me, I know deep down in my soul that this is only the beginning of the beautiful life we're going to have together.

We may have taken our time to find each other, but everything we've been through in our lives led us to this moment, in this field, in each other's arms. And there's nowhere else we were ever meant to be.

Because the Mountain knew what she was doing. Funnily enough, she always does.

# EPILOGUE 1
## NORA

*Five years later*

Five years ago, I was content with my life except for one thing—having a crush on one of my biggest clients and thinking of things that could never be. I didn't think a man like Randy Barnes would ever see me as anything other than his trusted accountant, let alone want to date a single mom with a rebellious teenage daughter.

But I couldn't have been more wrong.

And now, I can't imagine a life without Randy by my side, at my back, and in my bed every single night. He's my rock, my best friend, my confidante, my biggest supporter, and the owner of my heart, and every day I wake up with a smile on my face and determination coursing through my veins to make sure that I give him back everything he continues to give me.

"Mommy, mommy," a little voice calls out before a calamity of heavy footsteps stomp down the hallway and into the kitchen where I'm preparing breakfast. I turn and plant my feet just in time before our four-year-old son, Grady, and our three-year-old daughter, Holly, crash into my legs, hiding behind me before Leah runs into the room after them with a dinosaur roar.

"Save us from Leah-Rex, Mommy," Grady squeals while Holly just giggles, both of them watching Leah dramatically stalk toward them.

"I'm gonna get you, then I'm going...to...*eat* you!" she bellows, screams and shrieks filling the air. Then I'm laughing as the kids scamper out of the room and Leah huffs out a happy yet exhausted sigh as she slumps down into a kitchen chair.

She shakes her head. "I don't know how you keep up with them. I know I was a handful, but those two run me ragged, and I've got sixteen years on you."

I quirk a brow. "You calling me old, daughter dearest?"

"*Me*? Would I do that?" she says, feigning innocence.

Narrowing my eyes, I chuckle. "Yes, you. I swear having you home hypes the little cherubs up. They love their big sissy."

Leah's expression softens and warms. "It's definitely good to be home." Leah left home for college after high school and is now majoring in equine studies in Anchorage. When she moved there, we even thought it would be a fun throwback to all ride the train there with her—legally this time. She took it all in her stride though and continues to be the mature, responsible, level-headed young woman I always hoped I'd raised her to be. We all love it when she comes home on her breaks, though, and after this year, she's already arranged with Randy and Kendra to return home to the ranch to work the land alongside the rest of the family. I never thought I could be more proud of my daughter, but she continues to prove me wrong. She rents an apartment close to campus with Sage, and those two continue to be close. Wherever one goes, the other follows. They've even talked about living together in Molly and Beau's old rental—our old Kinleyville house—when they move back home. And having talked it through with Molly, Beau, Mom, and Randy, we all think it's a great idea. It'll still have the girls close to us, but with nobody cramping anyone else's style.

Even Mom moved into her own cottage on the ranch about a year after we moved in with Randy–bringing her boyfriend with her. It was a combination of her wanting to be closer to her grandbabies, but also for her and her *now-*husband, Stan–who is just as much the doting grandparent to the kids as Mom–to retire happily together.

"Any plans for the day?" I ask Leah as I pour her a cup of Ellie-Mae's cowboy brew, the recipe she graciously passed on to me when I became the 'woman of the ranch house' as she crowned me. She still comes over and helps me cook for everyone, but being the wife of the head of the ranch is a title that comes with responsibility, and one that I honor. The key to that is keeping my husband happy and relaxed and calming him down when someone annoys him. More often, it's Big Bruiser when he escapes the fence to get some loving from his latest cow girlfriend. I swear, that bull has the libido of *ten* horny bulls and seems hell bent on impregnating every female bovine within the ranch boundaries.

Leah takes the mug and cradles it in her hands, taking a long sip and moaning in delight. "Forget what I said. I *really* like being home because of this coffee right here."

I roll my eyes. "Gee, thanks, sweetheart."

"You're welcome, Mom."

"So, what are your plans for the day?" I ask her just as the kitchen door swings open and my sexy husband walks in, hanging his hat on the hooks, followed by the tall and strapping Colton behind him. The former teen crush, now filled-out rancher, dips his head and smiles at Leah before turning my way.

"Mornin', Nora. I just came to get a top up before headin' out to fix Bruiser's latest escape route," he says, earning a chuckle from Randy.

I look to my husband. "Again? What is that, the third time this month?"

"Yep," he says with a grin as he stops in front of me, wraps an arm around my waist and tugs me forward, pressing his curved lips to mine for a short but no less meaningful kiss. "Hey, darlin'."

"Hey." My reply is breathy, but I wouldn't have it any other way. My husband has that effect on me by just being in the same room, so it's nothing new for him to kiss me and have my body sparking to life.

When Randy lets me go to have a chat with Leah, I make quick work of topping up Colton's travel mug, not missing the way Leah's eyes track him the whole time, or how Colton seems to be avoiding her gaze. There's a story there, but Randy stayed true to his word that whatever there *was* between Colton and Leah as teenagers was taken care of and stopped before it could even start. When Leah left for college, Colton became a man about town. He works hard and is quite private about his social life around his family. He's never bought a girl home, but I do hear whispers about him dating here and there–but never anything serious. I guess he's behaving like the rest of Barnes men and biding his time until the Call comes his way..

I often wonder if there's more to the attraction between him and my daughter, because Leah has never seemed interested in relationships since then, either. But maybe that's just coincidence and I'm reading into things. As with all things, time will tell. Randy and I waited years before acting on our attraction and look how *that* turned out...

Ready to get back to work, Randy checks in on Grady and Holly before giving me a kiss goodbye and whispering promises of a long adults-only lunch break when he returns. Then he and Colton leave us with a smile and a wave, Leah's eyes lingering on the door well after they've gone.

I reach into the kitchen drawer and pull out a surprise I arranged for her.

"Did you know Aster came out with another book? Another couple hearing the Mountain's Call," I say, holding out the advanced reader copy of 'Cowboy Seeks His Girl' for her.

Her eyes widen before she squeaks with delight. "Yes! I knew this Mountain Spirit would look after me, even though I'm not a Barnes."

I tilt my head. "Maybe not by blood, but you *are* a Barnes now. Remember?" It was at our wedding reception that Leah and I gave Randy a special wedding present of our own—adoption papers so that he could officially become Leah's father. It's one of the few times I've seen my man speechless and a little teared up. I've never seen him sign his name so fast, either.

"Yeah," she says with a wry smile. She glances toward the door again before dipping her head down to the book in her hands, opening her mouth to say something before shutting it again.

"Sweetheart?" I ask, taking a seat opposite her.

Leah looks up at me, and I can see the conflict swirling in her eyes. "It's just... well...do you think *I* might hear the Call one day?"

I reach out and cover her hand with mine, offering her an encouraging smile because if there's anything I wish for Leah, it's exactly what *my* mom wished for me. Happiness.

"I think that anything is possible when you live on the lands of Eagle Mountain, sweetheart. The spirit is all-knowing and only She knows who is next and when the next Call will sound."

"And Kendra," Leah says with a snicker. "She always knows too."

"Yes. And Kendra."

"Love you, Mom. I hope you know that I'll never stop being grateful to you for not giving up on me."

Now it's my turn to tear up, but I do it without shame because this is what motherhood is all about, loving and teaching your children and then celebrating when you realize you did your job right.

"And I never will, sweetheart. I never will."

# EPILOGUE 2
## RANDY

*Ten years later...*

There comes a time in every father's life when he's forced to take a step back as the main man in his daughter's life. And when it's time for Leah to walk down the aisle toward her One not long after her twenty-sixth birthday, I find myself getting a bit choked up. Even though I knew this was coming, and I'm so incredibly happy for her, I can't help but see this as the end of an era. We've been through a lot together.

"Oh, Dad," Leah says, reaching up and running her thumb across my crows feet, trying to wipe the moisture from my tears away as I admire her in her gorgeous white dress. "If you keep cryin' like that, then I'm gonna start crying too, and then my makeup will be ruined."

"Just because I didn't become your dad until you were sixteen doesn't mean I don't feel like I'm losin' my baby girl here. You look so much like your mom," I whisper, my voice hoarse as I take her hands in mine. "So beautiful. We're both so proud of the woman you've grown into."

"Well, I wouldn't even be here if it wasn't for you coming into our lives. You made all the difference, and becomin' part of your family is what's led me to the start of a family of my own. And we won't go far, I promise. My heart is on this mountain just as much as yours is. This is an exciting new beginning for all of us, you know."

"You're not wrong about that. A beginning that I hope will lead to many more mountain weddin's blessed by the spirit herself." I lift my head as the bridal march starts up, scrub a hand over my face, then offer Leah my arm. "Ready, sweetheart?"

She slips her hand in the crook of my elbow and smiles. "As I'll ever be."

I lead her out of the small room we've been waiting in and down a short set of stairs that leads us right toward the purpose-built aisle where all the guests are waiting. The music is beautiful, and it's all I can do not to burst into tears as my biggest baby girl begins her walk toward her husband-to-be, a man who looks like he might pass out the moment he lays eyes on his bride.

As Leah nears her groom, my eyes scan our family and friends until my gaze settles on Nora, who's just as choked up as I am watching our girl get married, while she sits with her mother and Stan, and our other two children—all looking so proud and happy for Leah.

"I love you," Nora mouths, her hand to her heart while the other dabs a Kleenex at her eyes.

"Love you too," I mouth back, touching my chest before we reach the top of the aisle and it's time to begin the ceremony, starting with me–the bride's father–giving her away...

∽

"You know, I feel far too young to be the mother of the bride," Nora muses as I twirl her around the dance floor, long after the majority of the wedding guests have gone home. We said goodbye to the bride and groom hours ago, waving them off as they embark on a tropical honeymoon to start off their married life in style.

Beverly and Stan took the kids home not long after that, freeing my wife and I up to bask in the memories of our own wedding and happy life together. It's been a wonderful decade.

"You look too young, too," I say, grinning as I pull her in close and sway some more. "You're only forty-two, you know?"

"Hmmm, curse of being a teenage mother, I guess. When Grady and Holly are old enough to marry, I'll be in my sixties."

"Like me?" I tease, my arm sliding around her waist a little tighter so she's got nowhere to go.

"You are fifty-eight, Randy. You know how much I hate it that you keep adding years to your age. You've been telling everyone you're almost sixty since you were fifty-one."

Chuckling, I brush my lips against hers. "That's because it surprises them that I look so good for my age. Makes them understand how an old man like me managed to land a woman almost sixteen years my junior."

"Not that they'd know since you keep lying about your age."

"You know, the moment I turn sixty, I'm gonna start callin' myself seventy. So you may as well get used to it."

Pressing her hand against my chest, she leans back to look into my eyes; hers sparkling with laughter. "You know I've never cared about those years between us? You are my heart, my soulmate. And age will never change that. Even if people start to think you're my grandpa," she sasses.

"Oh, I know, darlin'," I growl, sliding my hand against the side of her face and bringing her in for a kiss that's just as intense, deep and long as the first ones we ever shared. "Bein' with you makes me feel like I could live to a thousand."

"Well, I hope that's true. Because there's one more thing the Mountain has in store for the both of us now that our oldest daughter is all coupled up with her very own mountain king."

My brow shoots up. "And what's that?"

"Twins," she says, looping her arms behind my neck as I stop dancing very suddenly.

"Twins?"

A grin curves her mouth as she nods. "Feel like you've got the energy for two more little ones?"

"The energy?" I laugh. "Oh my god, darlin'. I've got more than enough energy for ten thousand kids. You know how much I love makin' and growin' babies with you." Making a small gap between us, I place a hand on her belly and smile. "Two more precious bundles."

"And then we're done. OK?"

Chuckling, I gather her into my arms and scoop her off her feet. "OK. We can be done. As long as I still get to ravage you every day and night from now until the day the Mountain calls us back home."

Carrying her off the dance floor and toward the ranch house, she places a hand against my cheek and happily sighs. "That sounds absolutely perfect to me, Randy Barnes."

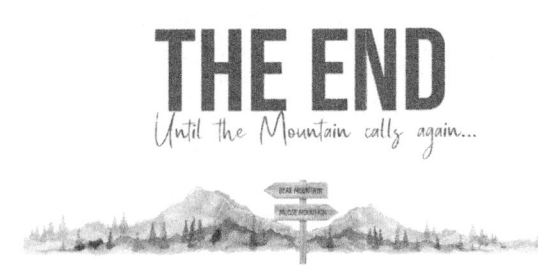

# THE END
*Until the Mountain calls again...*

...wait! How about a FREE mountain man book to tide you over? Tap this image or click the link below

*Marley Michaels*
when the mountain calls

Free book link: (newsletter opt in required)
https://dl.bookfunnel.com/h6c7b5gbl1

Annnnd don't go away yet. Cass's story is next in Cowboy Seeks his Queen. Tap the image and grab it here—>

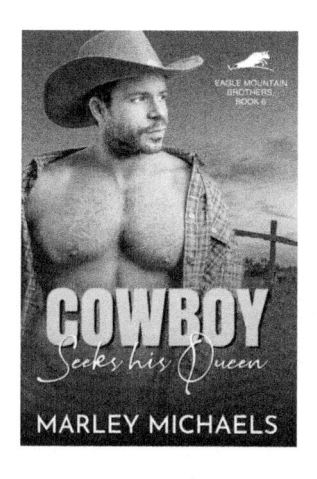

Sign up for my newsletter to receive release day emails: https://www.subscribepage.com/marleymichaels

Don't forget to add marleymichaelswrites@gmail.com to your address book!

If you're on social media, you can catch me on Facebook

https://www.facebook.com/authormarleymichaels/

or join my reader group

www.facebook.com/groups/856031968231022

Or you can follow me on Instagram

https://instagram.com/marleymichaelswrites

Can't wait to have more fun on the Mountains with you!

# MARLEY MICHAELS READING ORDER

**Moose Mountain Brothers**

Author Seeking Mountain Man

Introvert Seeking Mountain Man

Fangirl Seeking Mountain Man

Hiker Seeking Mountain Man

**Men of Moose Mountain**

Mountain Seeking Doctor

Mountain Seeking Pilot

Mountain Seeking Hero

Mountain Seeking Fire Chief

Mountain Seeking Veterinarian

Mountain Seeking Princess

Mountain Seeking Santa

**Bear Mountain Brothers**

Wallflower Seeks Mountain Man

Reporter Seeks Mountain Man

Artist Seeks Mountain Man

Baker Seeks Mountain Man

Dancer Seeks Mountain Man
Teacher Seeks Mountain Man
Runaway Seeks Mountain Man
Little Dove Seeks Mountain Man
Cowgirl Seeks Mountain Man

**Eagle Mountain Brothers**
Cowboy Seeks a Horse Whisperer
Cowboy Seeks a Romantic
Cowboy Seeks a Healer
Cowboy Seeks a Wild Child
Cowboy Seeks a Wife
Cowboy Seeks his Queen

Printed in Great Britain
by Amazon